MW00915420

Anthology:

The Collected Words of

Spoken Word of Mobile

A 20th Anniversary

Celebration

Mobile, Alabama

Welcome to Spoken Word of Mobile!

Spoken Word of Mobile Anthology

Collection Voices

An Introduction 1
The Spoken Word of Mobile Family 2
Memories 5
Dedication 6
Mrs. Sarah Hester Crawley Fields 7
Lorrena Blair 15
Theola Bright 25
Deidra Bloxton Craig 39
Emma Davis 47
Sharon Davis 57
Stacey Davis 63
Nikol Day 71
Willie Dinish Jr. 75
Latoya Dukes, MEd 85
Delores Gibson 89
Cassandra Sims Hansberrry 99
LaMya Hatton 105
Marlette Holt 117
Beverly Jo Jones 123
Cheryl "CJ" Jones 131
Gert Laffiette 145
Wanda R. Seals Lewis 153
Michael Norris 163
Nonnie Parker 179
Cynthia R. Poe 187
Tiffany Pogue 193
Daron Ray 201
Cassondra Sims 211
Sarah "BOAZ" Szejniuk 219
Geneo Williams 223
James Williams, Jr. 227

Welcome to Spoken Word of Mobile!

Spoken Word of Mobile Anthology

"SWM"

Spoken Word of Mobile Logo

An Introduction

Spoken Word of Mobile was established back in 2001 with the ideal of simply coming out, listening to, and reading your poetry. It was created with the sense of allowing people, individuals from the ages of 5 to 75 to come to a place where they could be expressive, to come to a place where they have creatively written their thoughts that turn into their poetic expressions.

Spoken Word of Mobile has had so many individuals come through the doors of the Toulminville Branch Library: some come in fear, some come in robust boldness as others just come to listen. Some are motivated to get up and read, be it their own work or the work of others. But the one thing that I can say about Spoken Word of Mobile is that it is a full feeling of a festive profound time of poets, of poetry, of spoken word, of experiences, of feelings, of thoughts and movements; it is the flow of our individual selves that come together as one in a room filled with words and expressions.

Spoken Word of Mobile is a place where once you have come, you are looking to come back. That is the environment that was set from day one that continues to flow as our days are unnumbered. The hope is that Spoken Word of Mobile can continue to touch the lives of people that can help to change and mold the accomplishments of their poetry.

As a wordsmith myself, there is so much that I have to say, so I have learned to put it down on paper so that others can hear it, so that others can read it, and right now, today, it is for you to have, our experiences, in the palm of your hands.

It is our hope that you enjoy the reading of our movements in Spoken Word of Mobile and in the thoughts of the poets of Spoken Word of Mobile. As the founder of Spoken Word of Mobile, it is my true hope and desire that you feel too what we share each and every month on the third Monday at 6:00pm.

Until next time, peace!

- **Cheryl "CJ" Jones**

The Spoken Word of Mobile Family

Spoken Word of Mobile

Pictured here are:

Delores Gibson, Sharon Davis,Latoya Dukes, Stacey Davis, James Williams,

Theola Bright, Geneo Williams, Cynthia R. Poe

The Spoken Word of Mobile Family

Spoken Word of Mobile Members

Pictured here from the left are:

Cassandra Hansberry, Cynthia R. Poe, Sharon Davis, "CJ" Jones, Emma Davis, Delores Gibson, Marlette Holt, Stacey Davis, Kaffy Griffin, James Williams, Metrulla Barnes, Theola Bright, Sarah Szejniuk, Geneo Williams, Mosi Ali

The Spoken Word of Mobile Family

Spoken Word of Mobile
Youth Poetry Slam-A-Rama

Spoken Word of Mobile hosts an annual Youth Poetry Slam in April of each year.

Featured are winners from approximate 2010.

And present are SWM Members from the left: Becca Horne (R.I.P.), Sarah Szejniuk, Theola Bright, Delores Gibson, Geneo Williams, Emma Davis, Marlette Holt, Sharon Davis, Stacey Davis, Lorrena Blair, Cynthia R. Poe, Gert Laffiette, Annie A. Evans

Memories

Honoring Those Members

Who Blessed Us

With Their Voices

Dedication

This project is dedicated in loving memory and

to the lovely memory of

Poetess, Sister Kaffy Griffin

Sunrise Dec 2,1952

-

Sunset June 21,2023

Spoken Word of Mobile Member

2017 - 2023

Mrs. Sarah Hester Crawley Fields

Sunrise March 9, 1923

—

Sunset February 10, 2010

Sarah H. Fields was born in Eutaw, Alabama March 9, 1923. Her parents were Theodore and Josephine Colvin. She had one sister Mazzerean Colvin Griffin. She was married to Irving L Fields for 62 years. She was the mother of 4 children: G. Douglas Crawley, Glenda Wall Fields, Irving Vincent Fields and Yolonda A. Fields. Ten grandchildren: G. Tony Crawley, Geoffrey Crawley, Ricky Motley, Sara Wall, Bennie Fields, Nigle Laddie, Terrence Fields, Charles Fields, Phylicia Reed and Preston Fields. Eleven great grandchildren: Adam Tapia, Langston Crawley, Miles Crawley, Aaron Motley, Morgan Motley, Terrence Fields Jr, Aiyanna Crawley and Taylor Fields, Cameron Laddie, Carson Laddie & Hudson Reed to great grandchildren.

Sarah Fields was a spry lady who was a senior member of the poetical group and was an enthusiastic member of Spoken Word of Mobile. Her poems ran the gamut from humorous to religious and left no doubt in the listener's mind that she was a great lover of the universe and all its phenomena. She enjoyed poetry night at Toulminville Library. Her love for poetry started at an early age, her 1st poem was written in 1934 when she was 11 years old. The last poem she wrote was penned the morning of her husband's funeral. And was recited at his funeral. She was a deep thinker and a great lover of excellence, beauty, the arts and mankind. She was an avid Scrabble player who loved words, books, English, knowledge, quiz game programs and music.

I Shall Not Have Lived In Vain
By Sarah Fields - 1947

A few days here upon this earth, A race to lose or success to gain

Will my existence worthy be or shall I live my life in vain?

I may even build a city, or discover some rich unknown land

I may chance to rule a country, and guide it with an iron hand.

Oh, I may do a many good things, on earth as far as man is concerned.

When judged by God, how great are we? Which deeds were really worthwhile done?

If I can help some weary soul, feel a little less lonely, a little less old.

God, give me the strength and I shall try, to save my fellow man until I die.

If my shoulders help to bear the burdens of some weary soul.

If one small piece of bread I share, or shelter someone from the cold.

If I help spread the word of God, to some stray ear, His word proclaim.

To just live on earth and be of service, then I shall not have lived in vain.

The Garden Party
By Sarah Fields - 1934

The Garden gave a party, one summer, Wednesday night.
The stars above were twinkling, and the moon was shining bright.

All vegetables were invited, and Oh Boy! Did they go!
Admission was a sandwich and a dollar at the door.

The lettuce made the lemonade. The okra fried the fish.
The turnip made the tomato soup. And gave them all a dish.

The cabbage played the piano. Oh how those notes did ring.
Miss Spinach sang a solo, as good as anything.

Everyone played checkers. Tomato won the game.
Mr. Pepper led in dominos, and Coon King just the same.

Cucumber did the Lindy Hop. The collards tried to trot.
The carrots jitterbugged a while, from the smallest one on up.

Miss Asparagus did the shagging. The beets did the Susie Q.
They all did the Big Apple. And said a poem or two.
Mrs. Pumpkin had a toothache. Mrs. Onion had a chill.
So her husband went to the drugstore to get her prescription filled.

Mrs. Rutabaga burned her new frock, now wasn't that a nice – to-do?

Mrs. Broccoli had to stay in bed, because she had the flu.

So these few failed to attend the party, grand and fine.

But swore by all the twigs on the trees that they'd be there the next time.

But everyone there enjoyed themselves. Yes, each and every one.

Remember the mighty Wednesday night, of barrels and barrels of fun.

At twelve o'clock they all went home, laughing with all their might.

And all they said was we'll meet here again, next Wednesday night.

By Sarah Fields - 1934

For Irving Fields 1924 - 2009
By Sarah Fields - 2009

He loved his church

He worked hard, He did for his family

What he thought was best

But when it all got too tough for him

The Lord just called him home to rest!

And when the time came, he didn't hold back

He answered the call as all good soldiers do

He had fought a good fight,

Irving we will always

Remember you.

Anthology:

The Collected Words of

Spoken Word of Mobile

A 20th Anniversary

Celebration

Lorrena Blair

Lorrena Blair was born in Mobile, AL. She attended Emerson Elementary School, Dunbar Junior High, and graduated from Central High School. Attended 20th Century Business College, The Branch (BSCC) School of Nursing. She was a professional medical assistant and lab technician for 25 years then she retired. She returned to work as a Family Service Case Worker for 11 years working with children three and four years of age. And has for the last 20 years used her trade and skills, knowledge and wisdom working as a substitute teacher at Craighead Elementary (Mobile County Public Schools).

Working with children is her joy, since way back in the old school. She once said, "I must be crazy working with 3 and 4 year-olds. But I guess I'm not. Working with young children is my calling. I believe that if I can help just one or two children as I travel along this way, I will then say my living isn't and wasn't in vain."

"I give God all the glory and praise and not man for whatever I have done to help anyone out of love."

She has been a member of Revelation Missionary Baptist Church for 34 years and is pleased to share that she is full of the Holy Spirit. Amen

Oh, Beautiful Lady
By Lorrena Blair

Oh, beautiful lady so sweet and kind. With your beautiful wide smile and kind heart; who loves everyone she meets. Oh! So kind, so giving of yourself; no matter what the situation may be. You handle it and deal with it with a big smile. God has allowed you to do that with a smile and you do it well; without a mumbling word.

Oh, beautiful lady, you are one of a kind when they made you so sweet, so kind, so giving and so loving to all mankind. They broke the mold because truly you are one of a kind. Such a beautiful, sweet, kind and giving heart; Lady continue the works that our Heavenly Father is allowing you to do, so that some little boy or girl, twin, young adults and older adults alike might say "I want to be like that." So beautiful, sweet, kind, great and caring Lady I call you a friend forever.

Keep holding on to your faith and to God's unchanging hand and whatever is a stumbling block in your life it shall be moved or you shall walk around it or over it in the name of Jesus. So, my beautiful lady so sweet and kind don't be burdened down about what man is doing. Because of your faith, the size of a mustard seed God has got it and you.

Humble you are and humble you shall receive with much love. So, continue to love. Love is what your Heavenly Father do in spite of and so do you.

- **By Lorrena Blair, 2014**

Mean Ole Me!
By Lorrena Blair

YES! They say I am mean; and I accept that with honor because I do MEAN what I say. Being stern with a child or children letting them know that you will not tolerate any MEANS of disrespect or talking back or mumbling then you are MEAN; then so be it.

Out of love, I speak; out of care, I give to all children. I do not click because it is a certain person's child (children). I give equally out of LOVE and not for show of man.

My work is of God who loves me so;
And my pleasing is to God not Man.

When I fall short after I have done my best; God will be there to pick me, his child up without question or complaint.

Oh God you are so awesome, caring and that is why I love you so much. So to those who think I am mean (I AM) and I applaud you for thinking so.

Until you see the villager is a helper and not a hindrance or MEAN; God have mercy upon you and maybe one day you will be grateful for the **"MEAN OLE ME!"**

OUT OF LOVE: YOUR HUMBLE SERVANT
Lorrena T. Blair, 07/15/2007

Oh! Beautiful Ladies of God
By Lorrena Blair

How wonderful you are and how beautiful you look. God is so good to us that he gives each and every one of us that special look and appearance. So beautiful ladies of God smile as you go along this beautiful journey of life; be happy and full of joy with lots of love for one another as our father have for us.

Spread love and show love everywhere you go. Along the highways and in your neighborhood and to those who are burdened down just a little more than you. Pray and ask God to give you the mind and spirit to reach out and help someone with love.

Oh! Beautiful ladies in your red and white and your lovely smiles; let us give thanks to God for all he has done; all that he is going to do in our lives not just for tonight but for eternity and forever. So, on this Valentine's occasion let us give God all the praise and glory for it all.

Oh! Beautiful ladies of God hold on to your joy and peace and most of all your love; and truly everyday will be Valentine's Day in your heart and soul. And to your better half, your fiancée or your significant other and friends and loved one, you hold onto these (3) three; joy, peace and love.

So, in closing to all you beautiful Women of colors in your Red and white and to your handsome guest and loved ones, "With God all things are possible." Tonight, we give God all the glory and praise for this beautiful evening and may God Bless and keep you all each and every day.

To all of our Sisters and Brothers in Christ we wish you a "Happy Valentines' Day."

On the Occasion of Valentines' Day
Your Humble Service of God
Lorrena T. Blair - January 10, 2006

Why Can't We Just Get Along in Jesus Name?
By Lorrena Blair

How can you sit there with a smile on your face and think that you are all of that and that the world is centered around you? Not so, not even in your dream or fantasy life; because it involves all of God's children and that is why I asked the question, "Why can't we just get along for peace sake?"

You know it's so much easier if we just love one another and reach out and help each other as we are blessed along the way. God loves a cheerful giver in every aspect in life if you see your brother or sister in need of a helping hand in any form of life; if it is just a kind word or a smile or just a hug to say, "I love you and you are not alone."

Give your all and all to do good toward others that your reward will be bountiful in heaven with your Lord Jesus Christ and not man.

If we live to show ourselves approved to our Lord and not to man trusting and believing that our God will see us through everything that happens in our life; if we just hold out and lean not to our own understanding but God's.

You don't have to know me to love me or show love because in doing so it shows the God in you. Do good and good will follow you. Do bad or wrong and it shall do the same.

So I say to you LOVE in spite of and give your all and all to do good toward your fellowman in everything; don't claw them down. SHOW LOVE!

Your Humble Servant
Lorrena T. Blair - 09/17/2007

"Every Smile is not a Friend but receive it with love."

Little Man
By Lorrena Blair

Little man, you are so short in stature; but a great giant at heart.

You are so giving and sweet spirited and a doer for mankind.

When asked or when you see something or someone in need you move and stand-up right-on time.

Keep on being the little big man you are; and the Lord knows it will pay off in time and if you hold on and out; your heavenly Father will reward you openly and abundantly,

So little man in stature and giant man at heart stay the same forever and to the end, you will see the good it was in doing so

Keep on giving your time and finish helping to stand up for the things that need standing up for.

Oh! So Great and mighty and humble you are, stay strong and mighty at heart forever giant. You are the greatest;

a friend indeed forever.

\-   **Lorrena Blair 2014**

Black Men! Black Men!
By Lorrena Blair

Black men stand up and stand your ground;

Black men! Black men stand for equal rights.

Black men if you don't stand up for justice that is equal, you might as well not stand.

Black men if you don't stand for peace and tranquility, we stand for nothing,

Black men, Black men stand, stand because if you don't who is going to go forth for our

little black boys and girls and all mankind.

If you all stand up together what a difference it will make;

Hold on to your brother and pull them up if you can, and not down.

It matters not if you like me, but Lord knows you are going to have

To love me to get to heaven. So let us stand up together because it is the

right thing to do. Our forefathers have worked too hard for us to go backward now.

Let us love an strive to the goal of success together holding hands and backing

each other up to the fullest; so that progress can continue on the road for equal

rights for all of mankind and not just some.

So Black men my continued prayer is that you all will put your trust in the Lord

and have no fear of man just God and that you will step up to the plate and take a stand

in the name of the LORD FOR JUSTICE AND EQUAL RIGHTS

Your Servant

Lorrena Blair 08/27/2013

God is So Good
By Lorrena Blair

God you are so good to us in spite of our sin and shortcomings.

I know you are in control of all that has taken place with your hurricanes, the wind, the rain, the flooding, the trees falling and the life you spared and shielded from all hurt, harm and danger.

I am mighty grateful to you for your goodness and your mercy that you had on these your children. God I thank you. My heart is full and my eyes are full of tears, sadness and joy; but as you said in Deuteronomy 32:39; It was in your hands and that all power is in your hand.

I know whatever your will is, it shall be; so we pray for everyone; that all shall be well in spite of their disaster; they will keep the faith.

I will continue to give you all the praise and glory that you are so worthy of. Out of all of the people that have spoken during the first several days of the disaster, none have mentioned God's name; but I know they have him in their heart. God, my heart is full and my hands are tied but my prayers are going on continuously; all through the day, every day.

Because I am a believer that prayer can and will change and fix everything for the good of those who love him, according to your faith in God. I know it has been said that the good and the bad have to suffer together sometimes but through it all he will bring you out.

But In that great gettin up morning the dead shall rise again and descend into heaven with their heavenly father. Oh! What a great day that will be. Your work left many homeless, many dead but in spite of it all you rode the storm and you spared us one more time. In spite of our sin you calmed the wind and the rain. You spoke the WORD and the storm stopped; along with "Peace Be Still."

Your Humble Servant
Lorrena T. Blair   9/2/05 – 9/04/05

Theola Bright

Theola Bright is a creative writer and publisher from Mobile, Alabama who is a former Artist-in-Residence for the State of Alabama. She is The Poet Laureate for Spoken Word of Mobile and a recipient of the prestigious St. Katharine Drexel Society Literary Award.

Theola is a presenter of Creative Writing Workshops, and the author of five books. She has published many books of children's poetry and prose for Miami–Dade Public Library for T C Bright Poetry Contest in South Florida, Mary B . Austin Elementary School in Mobile, The South Alabama Boys and Girls Club (Boot Camp), and Legacy 166 Summer School Program. She is a member of The Black Ink Coalition of African-American Authors, Mobile Writers Guild, Spoken Word of Mobile, and Phone Faith, which is a division of The International Recording Service for The Blind. She is also an actor, playwright and screenwriter.

Theola Bright is CEO and Founder of T.C. Bright Productions Ministry, Inc., a 501c3 non-profit organization that uses the Arts to promote the Good News Gospel. She serves the community in a variety of capacities and her works can be seen and heard at theolabright.com, YouTube or by Google search.

AFRICATOWN
By Theola Bright

A cloud of Knowing descended upon me
Covering me with a distance that sat me free
As it protected and reminded me to keep my candle lit
Knowing that I AM in this world but certainly not of it
Therefore, As I watch I also pray
To gain the strength I need to fight this battle each day
For I AM just a Sojourner of Truth only passing through
Watching the plans of old perdition unfold again as new
In a world of growing chaos that seems to be surreal
With corrupt systems within which are slowly being revealed
Knowing only the blind cannot see the obvious repetition
Of the stagnant water standing in the ditch of disposition
With the stench of his-story once again repeating itself
With no apologies for the eyes that cry for the lies heartfelt
My continence is wearing the face of a frown
As my heart bleeds today for the descendants of Africatown
No way for the right way except a Black way turn Blue Way
To fan the flies of pollution swarming underneath the Free Way
That is controlled by greedy hands for the Benjamins of commerce
That create these scenarios of surrealism again to be rehearsed
With more cuts and stabs in the back with zones in place of whips
And I can only stand here and cry with my hands on my hips
As I watch the Clotilde float by the Barracoons in my mind
To a place of gentrification that once was Africatown at one time
So glad AM I to just be passing through and not here to stay
Thankful that The Prayer of Serenity has sent me on my way
And here it is another Juneteenth and what have we to see
But broken down buildings surrounded by pollution and that old hanging tree

THEOLA BRIGHT
©June 7, 2022 for TCB Publishing
– First Printing Rights granted to The Spoken Word of Mobile Anthology - 2022

B-Right Bed and Breakfast House Rules
By Theola Bright

Breakfast is served between 6 and 9

Not after 10 or just any old time

This is not McDonalds that serves breakfast all day

And this is not Burger King where you can have it your way

Lunch and snacks you will have to prepare yourself

I don't have time to cook 3 meals a day for somebody else

They used to call this room and board but now it's called a B & B

Bed and Breakfast so any time I cook dinner for you - it's on me

I want to be through with all my cooking no later than 6

if you are not here when it's hot – a cold plate you will have to fix

Here's a key to your door so you can have some privacy

And I have a key to your door too because this is still my house you see

But I will give you prior notice before my entry

For inspection or repairs unless it's an emergency

No empty food containers and bottles cluttering up your room

because that will invite little critters to come here soon

Feel free to take your baths and showers

But I don't won't to hear the water running for a whole dang hour

I don't like dirty dishes in my sink

If you dirty up some dishes they will have to be washed by - who do you think

If you won't to hook up more than 3 electronics – please let me know

'cause my fuse box is on the outside and I sho' don't won't my fuse to blow

Now if you break something other than bread or wind

It's yours to keep because you done bought it, my friend

You've got to take responsibility for your actions - you see

At least that's what my mama always taught me

You are welcome to have visitors you can meet and greet in the parlor

But they can't spend the night even if they offer me more dollars

This is not the house that Jack built

This here is the house that the Lord built

And the Lord made me landlord and the Lord made me steward

I made rules to keep the peace that will make me happy if you do as you should

So these are the rules and I assure you I will be sweet

But if there is a rule you don't think you can keep

There is another B & B just down the street

And I won't be made at you

This will make me happy too

©Theola Bright - January 2020 for T C B Publishing

First Printing Rights granted to Spoken Word of Mobile Anthology 2022

"STOP THE VIOLENCE"
By Theola Bright

Statistics show that abuse and violence are increasing rapidly. Random and senseless killings have made the people reluctant to go shopping or attend events and large gatherings due to fear for their lives. The love of many has waxed cold and has caused hatred, indifference, and malice to breed in the minds and hearts of our children as well as adults. That hatred has grown into unexplained terror and violence as the majority sit in fear and silence complaining but doing nothing and saying nothing to help "**Stop The Violence.**"

STOP THE VIOLENCE

They started taking God out of the schools in 1964
And America has not been the same as it was before
1964 was a times when we did not have to lock our doors
Or put up iron bars from ceiling to floor
In our efforts to keep violence locked out as we are locked in
In fear as prisoners in our homes and temples within
Our world is filled with too much hate, terror and violence
That leaves our loved ones cold, dead, lying in silence
We have got to STOP THE VIOLENCE
By any means necessary
Before we all end up in a cemetery
We have been taught to "Train up a child in the way he should go"
But with no God in our lives how will our children ever know
That it is a sin to steal and it is a sin to kill

And that our purpose here is to love and do God's will
The lack of God's knowledge has caused a drastic change
with increased domestic abuse and pass the blame games
Of lies and deceit about the evil things done and the evil things seen
That corrupts minds with lyrics of music and scenes on the TV screen
We have got to STOP THE VIOLENCE
By any means necessary
We have got to STOP THE VIOLENCE
Before we all end up unnecessarily in the cemetery
-   ***RESOURCES: The Holy Bible - Matthews Chapter 24 Verses 3 through 15***

©**Theola Bright**

THANK YOU JESUS
By Theola Bright

(My Song of Praise)

Thank you Jesus I thank you Lord

Thank you Jesus from the bottom of my heart

Cause you brought me yes you brought me

From a mighty long way

Thank you Jesus I thank you Lord

Thank you Jesus from the bottom of my heart

For saving me

For healing me

For setting me free so I can be

All the things that you want me to be

Why should I fret

Tell me why should I cry

I have an awesome God

Who will not deny

Me anything I try

Or ask in prayer

He gave me the faith to wait

Knowing that He will be right there

Thank you Jesus I thank you Lord

Thank you Jesus with all of my heart

For taking my frown

Then turning it upside down

Oh how it makes me smile

Just to know that I AM your child

Thank you Jesus for walking with me

Thank you Jesus for talking with me

For taking my hand

So that I would understand

That I AM your witness

And it's about time

That I be about my Father's business

Thank you Jesus I thank you Lord

I thank you Jesus from the bottom of my heart

And now I AM preaching and teaching

Yes I AM singing and shouting

I AM trying my very best

To tell the whole wide world about Him

Thank you Jesus I thank you Lord

I thank you Jesus from the bottom of my heart

'Cause you've been my mother

And my father too

You've been my lawyer

When I didn't know what to do

I'm gonna tell it wherever I go

I want the whole wide world to know

That I thank you yes I thank you Lord

"Cause you brought me you know you brought me

Yes you brought me from a mighty long way

THEOLA BRIGHT

Taken from the book

"Just Thinking" – © 2006

Revised in 2022 for

Spoken Word of Mobile Anthology 2023

THAT STILL SMALL VOICE
By Theola Bright

One day I heard this voice

Speaking out from the crowd

And above all the noise

Giving me ultimatums

Yet leaving me the choice

To either set my own goals

do what I want to do

do it all on my own and

Struggle my whole life through

Or I could learn to listen

To this still small voice inside

That speaks to me as God's child

Giving me advice

For choosing a righteous way of life

Now I have learn to listen and to heed

The words I hear in my first mind

As I strive to succeed

Knowing the future is always near

When I hear that small voice in my ear

My one most important interjection

As I adhere without fear

Is to always strive for perfection

To be the very best that I can

To do as I am told

And to help my fellowman

As I listen to this voice

That comes from my soul

Giving me advice and peace

And strength for control

Even in a whisper above all the noise

I know when I hear my Master's voice

Taken from the book

Poems To Live By From The Soul of Theola Bright

© 1981 – T C B Publishing Miami Beach

Revised in 2022 for Spoken Word of Mobile Anthology 2023

WELFARE
By Theola Bright

WELFARE

Hell's fare

Just enough to keep us there

Machines have replaced the slaves

But the slaves have replaced no one

With no equal opportunity

No equal education

No 40 acres and a mule

With no reparation

leaves us as a race

Displaced and disgraced

And forced to face

WELFARE

Hell's fare

Giving us just enough to keep us there

A crutch disguised as a helper

A hand-out called food stamps

In a system designed to impair and control

The mind as well as the very soul

Of those who have learned

To do as they are told

Or be

Displaced and disgraced and forced to face

WELFARE

Hell's fare

Just enough to keep us there

Equal education and equal chance

Is the only way for a slave to advance

And what a threat we all could be

Should we every discover

Our strength in unity

And that we are not a minority

But a race displaced, then disgraced

And forced to face

WELFARE

Hell's fare

Just enough to keep us there

King Alfred's plan

Is a camp they call Hood

With chemicals, AIDS, COVID and bad food

Quarantine, drugged and then infested

Boys to men and then they are arrested

No more GOD in the schools

And no more golden rule

For a displaced race that has been disgraced

And forced to face

WELFARE

Hell's fare

Given just enough to keep us there

THEOLA BRIGHT

Taken from the book

"Just Thinking" ©2006

Revised for:

Spoken Word of Mobile Anthology - 2023

YOUR WEDDING DAY
By Theola Bright

The splendor of it all

Besides what you may recall

Is your reason for deciding to surrender

To an emotion so great

That this day and this date

By you will always be remembered

For today is your wedding day

A day set aside just for you

For your "something old, something new

Something borrowed and something blue"

A day to promise your love before God and man

To exchange a kiss and a wedding band

To share your love for the rest of your lives

Not as two, but as one

As husband and wife

Through the smiles and frowns

Through the joys and the let-downs

Through the tears and laughter

Here and now and even thereafter

In marriage you shall remain

_____and _____ sharing the same last name

As you remember to live up to your vows

By keeping love and forgiveness in your house

Then you will always stay together

Today – tomorrow – always and forever

THEOLA BRIGHT

Taken from the book

20 Years of Love

©2000 @ TCB Publishing

Deidra Bloxton Craig

Deidra Bloxton Craig Is the wife of Sanford Black Craig, mother of children Alisha Bre'Aunna Francis and Craig Maurelis Francis and Bonus son Sanford Black Craig II and six grandchildren Ailani, Charleston, Cameron, Zahara, Hazel, and Jordyn.

She has her Child Development Associates (CDA). She's an entrepreneur who operates and owns her own In-home family childcare facility, licensed through DHR, entitled Painting Healthy Habits for Creative Children Home Daycare, LLC. She's also in partnership with Auburn University Early Head Start program, and a member of (NAFCC) National Association for Family Child Care, Nationally Accredited and Quality Star approved. Deidra has been in the educational field for over 30 years.

Deidra is a member of the Spoken Word of Mobile, poetry organization, and she's a member of Delaware Missionary Baptist Church. She is the oldest of four girls to Sheila and Henry Bloxton. Her hobbies are painting canvases, journaling, and reading. Some of her favorite foods are spaghetti with beef and sausage and plenty of mozzarella cheese, cooked sushi, lemon pepper chicken, and Mexican tacos. She loves and enjoys being a part of the developmental breakthroughs that are achieved by her extended family through child care. Teaching children is a passion of hers, it gives her life.

I am an Alabamian
By Deidra Bloxton Craig

I am an Alabamian, sheltered in the surroundings of family in what appeared to me as a child to be a warm hearted state, crafted in diversity, a southerner, with countless traditions, made from the tapestry of my grandmother's quilt, sewing stitches, integrated fibers, living for something bigger than me. Books of old, antiques, a postage stamp collector, author and educator. I am Baptist, rooted in the religion. My life growing up was nurtured as a garden, sipping sweet tea, and lifting up the name of Jesus. Outdoor living in the spring time and summer sprinklers used for watering the gardens and keeping hydrated, while quenching my thirst beneath shaded pine trees. It kept me cool.

Oh yes, I am from what seemed like family reunions, weekly fellowships from the McCrea's, Blackman's, Bloxton's, Francis's and Craig's. It seemed like every Sunday meal served was certainly from the garden of the great one. With those fresh fruits and vegetables to the existing outdoor living room, surrounded around field peas, collards greens, and turnips, satsumas, plums, blueberries, watermelon, oranges and pears, even apple trees. I can smell my granny's, candy yams, collard greens, fried chicken, and meatloaf, not forgetting fried okra, fried corn, and her famous homemade buttermilk cornbread, with a tall glass of sweet tea.

Can't forget those homemade recipes, my favorite desserts my mother's german chocolate and red velvet cakes and her mother's sweet potato pies, it seemed like a constant family union of the Watts, McCrea's, Blackman's, outdoor living was to the family room, kitchen, dining room, indoor living room, to the company on the lanai sealed with loved ones from friends of the family, someone always came home invited by my granny to have dinner and fellowship.

The photos are priceless. I am from strict beginnings you know, I was always supervised and had to have chaperones, still hearing those embedded random family sayings you heard growing up, "young lady leave something to the imagination,"

" Careful who you hang around or to whom you engage with because associations brings on simulations", "My house is off limits to visitors while I'm not at home, the neighbors will be watching," "make sure you get a good education so that you don't have to depend on nobody." And I will never forget this one, "Hey! wash those hands before you touch my refrigerator."

I am from descendants of an entrepreneur spirit, an educator embracing gifts and talents that will be greater than me, passing this torch from generation to generation. I pray, yes, better than me for the greater cause for my future siblings and our society as a whole. I am of millionaire status. I receive it, I decreed it and declared it in Christ Jesus name Amen. I am all of who God says that I am.

I was always influenced to Imagine being greater, to walk effortlessly, conquering my goals, to tap into my dreams and was called Cinderella, a beautiful spirited character of hard work and seeing what's good in everything and everybody, I stayed prayed up, I had viewed that every lesson taught was connected to parables from the King James version the greatest book written: mine and my grandma's favorite inspirational advice, "speak that which is not as though it was," "write the vision and make it plain and seek God first", I was told, you have to always work hard to get your own and must be consistent, persistent in it and it shall come to pass."

Yesssss!

I am a true believer of it, because it all has impacted my life to make me who I am today. Yes I am from Alabama.

I am grateful! I am grateful!

I am an Alabamian.
- Deidra Bloxton Craig

A Prayer for Granny's Babies
By Deidra Craig

To my loving grandchildren. Every morning when you awake, I pray that you look to the hills from which your help comes from daily because all mine and your help comes from the Master.

The Maker of heaven and earth.

As long as you keep Him first He will never let you down, He who watches over you will not slumber. Know that in suffering produces perseverance and with perseverance makes up your character which brings you hope.

Know that the Lord watches over us all, He watches over your comings and goings, both now and forever more. Wait on the Lord, I say, I pray that you will be strong, take heart and wait on the Lord. Wait on His perfect timing. For it is He who gives us perfect peace. It's very important that you stay grounded in the Lord. Meditate and feed your spirit man daily with the reading of the word of God, know that you will be recognized by love, joy, peace, patience, kindness, goodness, faithfulness, gentleness, and self-control. They are the fruits of the spirit. Trust God.

Never let anyone bully you in making bad choices. Lead with the light you carry, it's Jesus! Remember, you are anointed. Speak only in faith where you know you're going, remember, faith, without works is dead, there is power in your tongue, keep speaking life over your soul, I want you to never betray your dreams. Make sure your dreams line up with the will of the Lord.

I want to thank God in advance for blessing you all to stand on His promises, and for allowing you to be a willing vessel for the good of change and the spreading of hope, fear not, God is with you. Know that we are self-confident in His confidence.

I pray that the Lord will use you all to make a positive difference in this world and in the lives of others. Do this for me, as well as for yourself recite-the Lord is my Shepherd I shall not want and believe it. I pray that Granny's babies keep a smile on the face of the Lord. It's in Jesus Christ's name. Amen□□

- **Deidra Bloxton Craig**

I Love You...
By Deidra Craig

I love you King Sanford,
I appreciate you,
for supporting my natural endeavors,
I see your intentions,
your positive disposition.

I love the way you maximize on our happiness.
I see you, I see you doing your best,
I'm so proud of you for being my better half,
Your actions show me that you do listen to me
And honor me and I you.

I love you, because of the respect
That you have for me
As your wife and Queen.

I thank God for strengthening
And keeping
A hedge of protection around us at all times.

I love you for all that you are, and all that I am.

My evolved man,
You are more than enough.
I promise to always find ways
To nurture and show love.

I admire your decision-making,
Your optimism and unconditional love.
May God continue to increase our union
Because the best is yet to come.
Love is in your face.
Tiamo.

-   **Deidra Bloxton Craig**

One of the Best Seasons…Glory to God!
Daily Affirmation
By Deidra Bloxton Craig

I am a child of the most High King

I believe that I can do all things through Christ Jesus who strengthens me.

I decree and declare that I will not sink, that I have stepped out of the boat of my past that I suffered in.

I am loved and I make room for those who respect and honor the Lord God and me as well.

God is my provider and has made provision for me. Everything I need is either in me or within my reach.

I am purposefully and wonderfully made. Glory to God!

My steps are ordered by the Lord, I walk in expectations of all my needs being met. I am followed by abundance. It belongs to me.

Freedom belongs to me. Peace belongs to me.

I am a good steward over what God has given me.

I'm surely not the same person that I was a year ago. I see myself evolving into a better version of me. I constantly see myself reaching my highest potentials.

Everything is aligning in my life. I have balance, I am disciplined, I am focused. I am confident in whose I am. I believe that all things work together for the good of those that love the Lord and are called for His purpose.I am self-confident and rooted in His confidence.I have stepped out of the boat.

I am confidently sure my troubles are over! I will not dwell on the hypotheticals I'm casting them all down in Christ Jesus name. Glory to God!

I have entered into supernatural rest that only comes from completely trusting in the Lord. Glory to God!

I am elated that I can be free to love and accept others rather than compete with or compare myself with them. I thank God for making me unique. Glory to God!

I am in one of the best seasons of my life! Glory to God! Amen!

- **Deidra Bloxton Craig**

The Power of Navel Oranges
By Deidra Craig

Mmmmmmmm!

The taste of acidic flavors,
Love is in the air,
a blanket of citrus blooms on the trees,
the aroma of navel oranges lingering in the air,
you appreciate the sweet seedless
and easy to peel navel oranges period.

In Africa,
the delicious navel oranges
are a growing popularity,
it's a South African summer citrus
which means fresh, sweet, juicy.
It's a crowd pleaser,
perfect for fruit salads,
juicing, baking, dressing up beverage glasses
and entertainment
during those hot summer months.

Ms. Bloxton has a city small farm
of citrus fruits in her backyard,
Donating buckets of citrus fruits
to her church, family and neighbors,
it's a real thirst quencher for most,
a healing drink full of vitamin C for others,
great for the children in every season,
because you and I know
It's very good for the immune system.

Big Mama starts her pruning in June
through the end of October.
However, in the late winter of December
until March
everyone starts to bring their buckets,
bags and empty containers.

It's Harvest time!

It's Harvest time!

- **Deidra Bloxton Craig**

Emma Davis

Mrs. Emma M. Davis is a native of Mobile, Alabama with a deep passion for the arts. She is a professional counselor, educator, and motivational speaker (with God's word on her lips). She is also a profound writer of songs, greeting cards, poetry, as well as children's books.

In her personal view, "I am an Academy Award winner of three children who graduated from middle school". She believes that once a child has matriculated from middle school, they have chosen a path. She is currently retired and continuing to serve the community through various volunteer avenues.

Bouquet!!
A Poem for Mrs. Clark
By Emma Davis

A bouquet of memories, on Chinquapin Street, "In the famous Bottom"
We celebrate with you and your magnificent family, on your 100th Birthday October 12,
2022.
"She holds a world of memories in her treasure chest of the favor from the Lord, while
she loves his people."

Mrs. Clark, I bring joy, expectations and Godly memories of my childhood, walking down
Chinquapin
Street and seeing Mr. Clark sitting on the front porch, and then you walked out, and that
is my first

memory of being in the presence of royalty.
The Queen of Chinquapin Street.
The Queen of the Bottom.
I am so blessed.
In all things give thanks.

From the entire McMillan family and friends, we are thankful to know you and have
heard of you.
P.S. The three churches on the block: The Baptist church, The Holiness Church and the
Clark's House.

Emma M. Davis
Mother, Author Poet

Going to the Wedding
By Emma Davis

She was born to love.

She learned how to dress for all occasions, fine and petite.

This was her.

Her children looked to her attires and desires to dress in life like her, and her grandchildren marveled at her.

All the flower girls are dressed in sweet colors of the flowers, sweet like the lilies in the field.
Her sisters and brothers knew their part in her life. Knowing she would say, would you like to go on my

honeymoon with us?

All of her preparations were put together well.

Then, she pulled the veil down over her face smiling so happy, my love has come to marry me.

My greatest joy was I am going to the wedding.

The wedding where she will meet her joy, turning to her father God to be with him forever.

I am at the wedding celebration of her new life with Christ forever.

Christ is her forever wedding partner.
In memory A. Ephraim

Emma M. Davis
Mother, Author, Poet

Hail to the Queen
A Poem for Aunt Fannie
By Emma Davis

Salvation has caused all of us to be here!
This Queen held the name of Jesus up for us all.

We give thanks to Father God for his love for us, and all the joy of family.

Aunt Fannie, was our Joy.
She took her place in prayer for all of us.
What can you save through prayer?

Everyone can look around and see the beauty in the power of prayer.

Aunt Fannie was our Matriarch.

She demonstrated so much power within us to speak to the mountains.

She walked by the word of God, she taught the word, and she moved in the power of prayer and faith.

Oh, did she love us all, yes, yes indeed she did.
Let us all remember how she loved us unconditionally.

We are the children of the late Albert & Stella, the grandchildren, great grands, on through the fourth

and fifth generations. What a blessing to see.

She was salvation, laughter, peace and joy in sharing, caring, and giving to everyone that she met.

We love you Aunt Fannie, our Queen!

Emma M. Davis
Mother, Author, Poet

I Awaken Again
By Emma Davis

My eyes opened. My heart sounded like the movement of a swishing washing machine, sure to get the

dirt out of the clothes.

I saw the light from the morning, so bright I knew then, I awakened again, hummm. I had nothing to do

with it, but I awakened again.

My mind started to move like an Amtrak train. My thoughts were racing fast, faster than a marathon

runner trying to be the winner, the first to the finish line.

My body rushing trying to catch up to some of my thoughts. Maybe there is something I need to fulfill,

hopefully I would finish the many things on my agenda in my mind for the day.

Because I awaken again.

You see, only because I awaken again, I can have this thing called life. Someone maybe put me to sleep
and woke me again, I really don't know but I heard there is a savior in whom I can believe.

I awaken again.

Someone said, maybe we should explore what caused the sun to shine during the day and the moon at

night causing the days to change because they awakened again too.
I am still here because I awakened again and that is the truth.

I awaken again.

"Before He made the world...God chose us in Christ." Ephesians 1:4

A poem to encourage those in the fight for their life medically, to keep fighting. I understand the

urgency to keep moving daily, because you are in a race for your life.

Emma M. Davis
Mother, Author Poet

Listen
By Emma Davis

A poem reflecting on a scheduled life of teachers retiring; a consistent Woman of God
that served
children over 35 yrs.
Shush, be quiet, stop talking.
Put your coat here, and this is your desk.

Ten years later....
Good morning, listen for your name.
Walk in a straight line.

(Twenty years later) Good morning, your work is on the board, follow the directions. I
am watching you.
Birthday parties, Valentine's Day, Christmas, and the end of the year. Parties for the
children that

should've been in the Guinness book of World Records.

Pack up, put things away, have a great summer, the school year has come to an end.
Before you know it spring flowers in bloom but the same remains true
Ok class sit up straight and listen for your name.
Pull out your book and turn to page 7, completion, "my joy is fulfilled."
Oh, the beauty in the Azalea's and all of the pastel colors.

Listen class turn to page 8.

Today is farewell, we will hold our memories forever. I did it all, I did it all, I turned to
page eight.

My new Beginnings!!!

Emma M. Davis
Mother, Author, Poet

Treasure of my Past
By Emma Davis

I did not want to give up my treasures.
I didn't want to give them up, because they were mines.

They are all mines.
He was my treasure.
He was my sunshine.
He was my joy.
He was my love.
He is my memory.
My all in all.
He was my train driver.
He was the conductor too.

These are my memories that we shared together.
They were to keep me cozy at night.
My treasure, the well lived life of "Love."

My treasure will keep me warm in the winter breeze, sunny as the flowers blooms in the spring.

Summer, just fun!

Fun so much you will never know how much.

My treasures.

I will hold on to them because they are just for me.
Then I realized who is this world traveler?

He belonged to me, but yet it was the adventure in his eyes, that made me understand that he belonged

to the world.

He shared his love to everyone he met.
He shared his knowledge.
He shared his skills.

He shared his wealth and his wealth of wisdom.
His wisdom was beyond our knowing, so wise.
He was an "Open Friendship Train."

Tell the world, the ones that did not know him, what a treat they missed.

He was a friend of Jesus, and a treasure to the world. Let the world know that he was a friendship train.
We rode with him, and his joy was to show us the love of Jesus, and he did it well!

"Mr. Love, a Friend of Jesus."
Thank you for letting us meet him....
Mr. Love: The Friendship Train what a ride,
"What a ride" A friend indeed.

Thanks always for your love and the attention you showed us.

Emma M. Davis
Mother, Author, Poet

Sharon Davis

"Strong Woman"

Sharon is a resident of Mobile, Alabama. She is a proud mother of one son and three grandchildren. Her hobbies include reading mystery novels, working jigsaw puzzles, and writing poetry.

She started writing poetry when she was in middle school. When she writes poetry it expresses the depth of her emotions and her ability to relate to people on a very personal level.

Her poem "Strong Woman" radiates power, confidence and strength that women need to be more resilient and more independent and to never give up on their dreams.

Nobody Can See Through Your Eyes But You
By Sharon Davis

I often think of the words of wisdom my mother gave me.
Not realizing that one day they would save me.
When I wouldn't listen and I'd say within my heart:
"You're lying. None of what you're saying is true!"
Her last words would be:
"Nobody can see through your eyes but you!"

As a child she took me to church, taught me "The Lord's Prayer,"
"23rd Psalm,"
"Birth, Death, and Resurrection of Jesus," and "The Golden Rule."
But then I didn't have a clue:
"Nobody can see through your eyes but you!"

I went on about my business doing things I shouldn't do,
saying things I shouldn't say, and going places I shouldn't go.
"I'm grown," I'd say. "What does she know?" "I know what I'm doing,
She can't tell me what to do!"
That little voice would say:
"Nobody can see through your eyes but you!"

I made mistakes. I fell. I got up. I did right, I did wrong.
Sometimes I was up and about all night long.
I did everything I was big and bad enough to do. But still:
"Nobody can see through your eyes but you!"

I had to learn what these words meant.
At the time they didn't make much sense.
I've learned that you have to look at things differently.
You have to use your heart, not just your eyes to see.
I thank God for giving me a mother who could tell.
That someday I would learn what she already knew:
"Nobody can see through your eyes but you!"

@Sharon Davis

I AM A STRONG WOMAN
By Sharon Davis

I know that I can make it
Whatever the problem I can take it
I am a strong woman
I've gone through a lot
I've stood firm I'm leaning on the
Faith that I've got!

I am a strong woman
I've given my God my all
I can go through the fire I know he won't let me fall
Being strong is not just physical,
It's also a state of mind.
There are things that I have to learn, but, I'll grow
Stronger time after time!

There are those who are unhappy, and all they do is
Complain, I stay away from those sad faces, they
Would make me go insane!

I am a strong woman
I won't let things get me down
I'm free from the pressure of the world
I have a smile where there use to be a frown
God is my refuge: he gives me the love and support I
need. He's my guide and my protector, in his word I do
Believe!

I am a strong woman
My mind is free from daily worries
I take my time I'm no longer in a hurry
I thank god for his deliverance; he put me on the right
Path!

I am a strong woman: from this day until my last!!

Written by: Sharon Annette Davis

Prayer Is the Answer
By Sharon Davis

Prayer is the answer, prayer is the key;
Prayer will help people like you and me.

When you pray, pray with a sincere heart.
Pray honestly, truthfully, and faithfully,
God will give you a brand new start.

Prayer is the main contact we have with Jesus Christ.
Prayer will help you do what is right.
Prayer will give you courage to go on when others may stop and
Rest.
Go on with faith, God knows what's best.

Pray for guidance when things aren't too clear.
Pray when you're down and out- -
God is forever near.
When you're lonely, when you're blue,
Pray to Him, He'll help you.

Prayer is His way of keeping in touch with people of this Earth.
Pray to Him every day, He'll give you a brand new birth,
Prayer is forever, just like God's love.
Prayer will take you to live with Him above.

Prayer is the answer, prayer is the key;
Prayer will help people like you and me.

Sharon Davis

Copyright @2003 Sharon Davis

Your Grace and Mercy
By Sharon Davis

Dear lord I thank you you've been so good to me not
Only do I love and honor you I am grateful to thee

Dear lord I know that I am not perfect I sin against
You every day not just by my thoughts and deeds,
Also some of the things I say

I know that I am blessed and it's all because of you if
You had not saved me, I wouldn't know what to do

Throughout my life you've kept me even when I didn't
Know you were there you've been my guide and
Protector and I am always in your loving care

I don't deserve your love especially when I do wrong
You let me know that I am forgiven and to you I will
Always belong

You've cleansed my heart and mind from all my sins
And shame thank you for your grace and mercy & I
Praise you in Jesus name

Thank you father I have so much to say to you I know you know my heart and soul and
you've given me life
Anew

Lord I thank you for your grace and mercy I thank
You night and day dear lord I thank you in Jesus name
I pray…………………………………….
amen………………………………..

- **Sharon Davis**

Stacey Davis

"Lady Poet"

Stacey Davis is a wife and mother of three loving son's. She has always dedicated her life to healing and helping others and that is why being a nurse gives her joy.

Poetry fell in her lap at an early and sad time in her life with the passing of her mother. Poetry became her life line. Allowing her to breath and self heal. She likes to think that her Poetry was locked in her soul and now has been released. She has been a member of Spoken Word of Mobile for 18 years and counting. Sharing her gift gives her peace. She has written one book " Me Myself and Poetry" Pain, Love, and hope.

Flava
By Stacey Davis

We as black women come in all shape, sizes, and flava's.

Chocolate

Carmel

Mocha

Toffee

Cocoa

Butterscotch, and

Deep chocolate swirl.

Any flava a man wants, we're everywhere. We should be treated like the queens we were born to be, but half the time we're passed over for a vanilla milkshake, Too thin and all wet. I think these brothers have forgotten what a

Chocolate

Carmel

Mocha

Toffee

Cocoa

Butterscotch, and

Deep chocolate swirl Sista taste like.

I believe we need to seek these brothers out and give them just a little taste. Maybe even show him what a real Sista of flava can do when she is determined. We are irresistible in every way. All men regardless of race, want an experience with a true black goddess.

We melt in your mouth and not in your hands and make a man holla her name when she is done. A true backbone to her man and smart too. We take care of business in every way.

All men, not just a few. Will learn to respect a CHOCOLATE

CARMEL

MOCHA

TOFFEE

COCOA

BUTTER SCOTCH AND

DEEP CHOCOLATE SWIRL

QUEEN LIKE MYSELF!!!

- *Stacey Davis*

Cravings
By Stacey Davis

It's like a drug in my system, I just can't seem to shake.
Every hour on the hour it's calling me

"Staaacccey, Oh just one itty bitty taste for me please"

But I say no!!! I can't do it.

I promised, and I always keep my promises

Hands sweating, mouth watering, mind playing tricks on me. I don't know how much more I can take.

Staaacccey, "Oh don't I please you, make you feel good, don't I satisfy your hunger to taste"?

I beg "Please Stop".

But my hunger for you still haunts me

I Try to replace you with everything, still your calling, enticing me with my need to have you.

Staaacccey "Oh don't fight, take me" SOOOOOOOOOO!!!!!

Before I knew it, my hands were everywhere, grabbing, tearing, and pulling, Right into my mouth.

DAMN YOU CHOCOLATE!!!!!!!!!!!!!!!!!!!!

- *Stacey Davis*

Voices
By Stacey Davis

Who is that man behind that voice
Shaking me, Baking me
Making me ohhhh!!!

Who is that man behind that voice Shying

me, Trying me

Grinding me so

Who is that man behind that voice

Soothing me, Losing me

Making me glow

Who is that man behind that voice

Stopping me, Dropping me

Letting it flow

-   *Stacey Davis*

History
By Stacey Davis

She says I should be great

I was born this way

I was crowned by God as the queen of my race.

I am beautiful

I am black

I am African

I am negro

I am Queen

She says great women have walked this earth before me.

Strong, respectful, honored, and courageous, black Sista of history.

Their past has molded my future, my destiny on this earth. It is my turn you see, I

was crowned by God.

She says we have forgotten our Queens of the past and their struggles.

Harriet Tubman, Sojourner Truth, Mary Bethune, Coretta Scott King, and Shirley Chisholm, the first black female to run for president but pulled out. The list goes on and on black women of history. we thank God for giving our black men the wisdom and the knowledge needed to fight for equal rights for all mankind. We have since forgotten the women who fought alongside them, give them some respect.

Young women today have forgotten that they are true queen's by right. It has been written in the bible that our father is the King of all kings and we are his children.

She says be proud, show pride, hold your head of high young queen's because one day the future will need a strong, respected, honored, and courageous black women because

We were born this way. We were crowned by God as the queen of our race. We are beautiful

We are black

We are African

We are negro

We are Queens by right

BLACK WOMEN OF HISTORY

- *Stacey Davis*

Moves
By Stacey Davis

He has mesmerized me by the way he moves
to see him move brings chills to me,

Not the perfect man of course
but still his moves intoxicates me.

Dred's long and thick moving left to right and right to left with the sway of his body
when he moves.

The swaying entices me to move closer, but I dare not disturb the rhythm.

So graceful he moves with such passion and skills, I close my eyes to feel what he
feels when he moves.

Swaying and moving, in that hypnotic way.

Not once did he touch me or say any words,

he just kept moving, and swaying hypnotizing me.

\-   *Stacey Davis*

Nikol Day

Nikol Day was born in Cleveland Ohio. She is a 2019 University of South Alabama College graduate. Having a passion for people, she studied Human Resources. After earning her bachelor's degree, she began working in her local community. Remembering in her high school years, the poetry at the Toulminville Library. With great enthusiasm her intentions to support her local community became even more driven after accepting the invitation last April 2022, into membership for Spoken Word of Mobile. Hosting literacy workshops at the Dauphin Island Parkway Mobile Public Library. Crafting with school age children is lots of fun. As the Founder of Citi Poetry Outreach Platform promotes reconfiguration of social literacy.

Inspiration is found in the reflections and considerations thought. I find being present makes the experience. It's challenging to compartmentalize during moments but give it your full attention.

Spoken Word and Me
By Nikol Day

It was 2009

This place was God's sign

A free therapy home

For the internalized challenges trap n the dome

Hurt too thick to detangle with a comb

A warming inviting tone overheard lead my curiosity

With arms open a soft spoken woman greeted me

"Come on child take a seat" said Mrs. Laffiette

Soulful inspiration set the atmosphere

Sharing and bearing truths making the mind clear

Real poetry lives here

Undeniable Vision
By Nikol Day

2 lite windows with smudged splattered paint stained glasses offer a view of various green
shades Leaves dance to the amphoteric breeze
Bright orange leaves fall along with pine straw
Such scenery leads the mind into daze of a cozy cottage style home with bay windows
On the day bed resting with eyes cast upon botanical forestry
The leaves and trees beken exploration
Speaking iridescently to behold the full vision before mine eyes to see past the greenery
Examining the direction of nature
Noticing the upward growth
Branches reaching towards the sky
Even the smallest flowers rise to stand
Posing the question of is nourishment the purpose of the plan
Could mankind consider the nature of nature nourishes to live

Cultivating Creativity Collectively

Advantageously Aspiring

Together Teeming

Hemming Harmony

Admired Adaptation

Raises Rapport

Synthesizes Serenity

Inveterately Inspiring

Salubrious

Catharsis
By Nikol Day

Willie Dinish Jr.

Willie Dinish, Jr. is a native of Mobile, AL. He is a proud US Air Force veteran having served over 20 years, retiring with the rank of Technical Sergeant. During his time in the military he traveled the world and began writing to fill the hours of his travels.

He is the author of two books; one work of fiction, *The Quiet Mind* and one poetry collection, *Thoughts*, both of which are available on Amazon and other websites.

Remember
By Willie Dinish Jr.

I remember the feel of your heart,
The touch of your soul
The feel of your body
I remember

I remember the days and nights
That the earth stood still
As my arms held you close
I remember

I remember the journeys to a place
Close to heaven
As we stood and watched the world about
I remember

I remember the future dreamed
And life looked forward to
I remember

I remember the things accomplished
When two worked as one,
For a strong foundation was built and made
And things cannot be taken away
This too is true
I remember

I remember the world and life
Has many bumps and bruises
But love, true love
Will kiss and hold tight, remember this
I remember

Willie Dinish, Jr.
From the book <u>Thoughts</u>
Reprised with permission to the
Spoken Word of Mobile Anthology
© 2018

Because
By Willie Dinish, Jr.

Because your heart should know
I am the one that stands by you when sick or well

Because your heart should know
I say a prayer for your safety each night

Because your heart should know
I am the person that belongs by your side

Because your heart should know
that together we are blessed

Because your heart should know
that I won't for your love in my life

Because your heart should know
I love you in my arms, you make me whole

Because your heart should know
it's not what I can do or what you can do,
but it's what we can do together

Because your heart should know
that love is from the Lord
and the Lord has brought us together with love.

**Willie Dinish, Jr.
From the book Thoughts
Reprised with permission to the
Spoken Word of Mobile Anthology
© 2015**

Beautiful Woman
By Willie Dinish, Jr.

Beautiful woman love of my life
Come stand by my side forever
In life, joy and happiness

Beautiful woman love of my life
Know that my heart is
With you forever

Beautiful woman love of my life
Stand close and let our lives
Be one forever

Beautiful woman love of my life
Hear the sound of the world
As it sings of your happiness
In each others arms forever

Beautiful woman love of my life
Feel the joy of being
Near to each other
And helpmates forever

Beautiful woman love of my life
Come dance and laugh and smile
As the days turn into years
And time is our friend forever

Beautiful woman love of my life
Do not be afraid of the future
For we are that love
That will last forever

Beautiful woman love of my life
Love me forever
For I am the man
Who will love you
To that which beyond forever

Beautiful woman love of my life
Be the love that lasts for always
Be the love that shines and gives
Happiness to my world,

Be the love that
Holds my heart
Until the end of time

Beautiful woman love of my life
Let me not stand in love alone
Take my hand, hold my heart
And be in my life forever

Beautiful woman love of my life
Let the world sing of our love
As our future is seen by others
As made in heaven and blessed
By the Lord ever

Beautiful woman love of my life
See the light that glows
From my smile when you are near

Beautiful woman love of my life
Know that my heart beats to hear
Your voice and to know you are near

Beautiful woman love of my life
All I won't is to share this world
With you in my heart and
By my side for all days

Beautiful woman love of my life
Faith in the strength of our love
Through which we grew into a family

Beautiful woman love of my life
Have faith once again with love
Have faith in this heart
That beats to only you,
A heart that is full of love
Through which all things
Are possible

Beautiful woman love of my life
Have faith,
Love this heart,
Love this man,
Forever more

Beautiful woman love of my life
I have looked for the woman
That would change my life forever
A woman who would make me complete
A woman that would make me come to know
That I am blessed,
A woman that makes me smile
Through all days and nights
A woman that would take my breath away

Beautiful woman love of my life
Each morning, happiness greets me
As my alarm goes off to the song
Dedicated to my love
As it sings you take my breath away
And you have my heart
For all time
And you really do
Take my breath away

Beautiful woman love of my life
Hold this heart close to yours
As I pray for each and every day and night

Beautiful woman love of my life
Know that my love for you
Is that love that has no bounds,
Let this love be that love that
Love that lasts until the end of time
We are stronger together as one
Be one with me for always
So our love will be one

Beautiful woman love of my life
Hear the beat of my heart
It says love me forever

Beautiful woman love of my life
Hear the thoughts in my head
They say love me forever

Beautiful woman love of my life
Know that you have touched my soul
Love me forever

Beautiful woman love of my life

Be by my side as time goes by
And love me forever

Beautiful woman love of my life
My heart, head, soul and life
Misses you daily
Be my love forever

Beautiful woman love of my life
Look into these eyes
And see that they carry love
For you and only you

Beautiful woman love of my life
Read my poems and know my thoughts
Are of love
For you and only you

Beautiful woman love of my life
Please spend the rest of your days
With me for I love
You and only you

Beautiful woman love of my life
Grant me peace
Grant me love
Grant me happiness

Beautiful woman love of my life
Grant me the keys to your heart
That I may knows these above
And live with you in paradise
Forever

Beautiful woman love of my life
My heart is that which you have,
My love is part of me that I wish to shart
With you always
My life is filled when are near
Hold my heart, share my love,
Be in my life
Forever as my wife

Beautiful woman love of my life
I apologize for finding

You to be the woman
Of my dreams

Beautiful woman love of my life
I apologize for finding
That the world in better
When I am near you

Beautiful woman love of my life
I apologize for cherishing
Your mind, body and spirit

Beautiful woman love of my life
I apologize for won'ting
To give you all that I have

Beautiful woman love of my life
I apologize for my wish
To make you my wife

Beautiful woman love of my life
I apologize for this love
For you that will
Last forever

Beautiful woman love of my life
I apologize for not knowing
My making you happy
Would be so hard

Beautiful woman love of my life
I apologize for won'ting
To be by your side
As friend, helpmate,
Soulmate, husband
All that I can be

Beautiful woman love of my life
I apologize that you
Don't miss or love
Me as I do you

Beautiful woman love of my life
This day as all days
I think of you

Beautiful woman love of my life
This day I miss you
Today as of all days

Beautiful woman love of my life
I love you this day
As I do on all days

Beautiful woman love of my life
I look to you today
As I do all days
Be my wife
Share my life always

Beautiful woman love of my life
Come fill my mind
With thoughts of life
We shall have forevermore

Beautiful woman love of my life
Come fill my arms
With your warm embrace
From here and evermore

Beautiful woman love of my life
Love me, care for me
Hold me tight
From here and evermore

Beautiful woman, love of my life
My heart misses that beat
When it's not near you
My walk misses its step
My mind gets cloudy
And misses you daily

Clear my mind with the sweetest of your smile
Steady my steps with a touch of your hand
Make my heart beat as strong as forever
By the presence by your love,
By you being in my life for always

Beautiful woman, love of my life
The sight of you thrills my eyes
The sound of your voice is pleasing to my ears
When my heart feels you near its beats

Are stronger

Fill my life with your sight, let the sound
Of your voice bring pleasure to my eyes
Give my heart the strength to live forever
With you, fill my life make me happy
Be my wife

Beautiful woman love of my life
Be the center part of my life
Be my wife,
Be the joy of my morning
And my night
Be my wife,
Be the quiet
At the end of a hard day
Be my wife
Be the peace and happiness
That I lay my head
Next to as I sleep
Be my wife,
Bless me
Be my wife

**Willie Dinish, Jr.
From the book Thoughts
Reprised with permission to the
Spoken Word of Mobile Anthology
© 2017**

Latoya Dukes, MEd

Latoya Dukes formally known as Latoya "Liberty" was born in Pascagoula, Mississippi and raised in Mobile, Alabama. Among her parents and five siblings, Liberty expressed interest in music & writing at a very young age. She was able to express her feelings through the ups and downs she had experienced as a young girl. As a young rapper, Liberty wrote her way through John LeFlore High School and Bishop State Community College, where she participated in musical, poetic and art events around her.

She always enjoyed teaching, tutoring and spending time with family and friends. While attending the University of Montevallo, she and her husband met at a Spirit and Truth Ministries Church, produced Gospel music CDs and traveled for years. After graduation at University of Mobile and 15 years of marriage, she was blessed to have children, one girl and a boy. She shares with her family and friends the hope and peace that only God can give.

Today, she's a singer/songwriter and poet who loves to inspire. As a teacher, she encourages students in reading, writing and creativity. She believes that walking in faith, service above self, and embracing God given purpose is the key to success!

Matter's Most
By Latoya Dukes

When the color of skin is factored in with false accusation, that's when I clearly see such an untoward generation. Sadly, when mothers can't sleep at night for the fear of their child, and societal threats that hinders such a one from walking more than a mile. The economy is at a low and values are compromised and young ones are confused about what's considered a healthy lifestyle. One may say why is it important to attend church and gather with believers ? Why be modest when I don't feel my best to do either? Why work to become better when even the best is not embraced? Why hope for a better tomorrow when reality slaps you in the face? It's time to stretch toward the mark and reach again for what is biblically embedded. Remember Jesus and the Cross and those who came and went and never ever forget it.

- **Latoya Dukes, 1/18/13**

When Victory is in a Name
By Latoya Dukes

When Victory is in a name, the enemy stumbles at his task

When walking in faith, no derogative questions asked..

No counterfeit can seduce her to make her doubt her role.

Not a demonic entity dwelling inside a soul.

When victory looks in the mirror, she is pleased with God's creation.

From head to toe she know she's blessed with no alterations.

Without a struggle she shines brightly giving glory to her King, while

Singing softly in her heart and commits to publishing.

When victory is in a name those who are not aware

Allows the enemy to confuse them into thinking that they are getting somewhere,

Especially, when they go up against a child of God

Out of anger, ignorance, or because the path they chose was hard.

The pressures that surround the circle can cause one to retaliate.

It can bring about division, confusion, animosity and hate.

But when victory is in a name one rejoices in answered prayers.

Love and forgiveness is shown because she know who to cast her cares.

Jesus is more than a burden bearer, in fact, vengeance belongs to God.

For the battle is not mine's, and Victory is the Lord's.

- **Latoya Dukes, 7/4/14**

Revival
By Latoya Dukes

The satire from the new school mimics the old. The old black church for them had too much"soul." The dancing, the shouting and long hours of celebration. The rejoicing of King Jesus and His awesome salvation. Doing the kind of dance that doesn't care if you look and singing the kind of song that has only one hook. This experience doesn't compare to a night in the club. Where all kinds of beverages are sold and underage indulge. Unlike the club, the church doesn't have an age restriction. You can be of any race or age as long as you didn't leave out the same way you came. Which meant you were not listening and please come back again. This type of change brings joy and peace. It brings new life and faith levels increase. A greater hope for things to come reach the clouds. Prayers touch the heavenlies clear and aloud. The things of the past turns old and gets wiped away. And are remembered no more to this day. Charity spreads abroad like a sudden epidemic. People of different races gather together in unity with a vision and mission. God's name is exalted instead of prestige and titles. Back to back services turns into what we call a "Revival!"

- **Latoya Liberty Dukes, 7/9/13**

To God be the Glory

Delores Gibson

"The Barefooted Poet"

Delores Gibson resides in Mount Vernon, Alabama, with her husband of 40+ years. She is the mother of three lovely daughters. She's also a grandmother and loves spending time with family and friends. Delores is a member of the First Missionary Baptist Church in Mt.Vernon Al, where she taught Sunday school for many years. She believes in the power of prayer, her faith is her daily vitamin.

Delores is a poet, storyteller, playwright, monologist, and she even tries her hand at acting. She began bringing stories to life at an early age by using her vivid imagination. Her siblings and cousins were her audience. They clung to her every word. She now shares her work on many platforms, such as universities, schools, nursing homes, churches, open mics, art galleries, and festivals. She has also written and read poems for weddings as well as funerals. Her signature piece is BUCK, a story portraying the cruelty of slavery and the will to survive. Delores is a member and the vice president of Spoken Word of Mobile. For her, this is not just a pastime but a passion. With her bare feet, she will step to the mic and take you on a journey

Delores J. Gibson

The Barefooted Poet

To God be the Glory

The Barefooted Poet
By Delores Gibson

I got a thought in my brain and a word in my mouth,

and I want to be heard,

for I'm the Barefooted Poet.

I'll stand flat-footed and barefooted.

Talk to you real, tell you like it is.

I talk about Delores; I talk about the Lawd.

I talk about the cross and I talk about the crown.

I tell about the old and I tell about the young,

and from everywhere they come from.

I talk about Satan, for he is the real enemy.

I talk about my momma,

Pearl, and my three girls.

I talk about the motherland,

the harsh trip on the slave ship.

The cotton fields, Dr. King, and the Georgia hills.

I talk about education, segregation, and integration.

I share my Christianity, my love for GOD and humanity.

My words are not big, elaborate, or long.

They are simply my stories, simply my psalms.

I talk about it all from A to Z.

I'm The Barefooted Poet, that's me.

Delores J. Gibson
The Barefooted Poet

EMERGENCY
By Delores Gibson

I kick around words like raw herbs naturally,

I don't dot all my I's or cross all my T's

"Please"

Making my way to stage

I feel like a

ROOOAAAAARRRR!!!

Tiger in a half open cage,

I want to get out.

I spit poetry, prose poems with similes, metaphors, and hyperboles.

I share psalms like 23 and 91.

I share monologues as I move my jaws,

I can't help myself.

Writing whispers, paper crumbling,

Garbage filled with unfinished lines

Trying to make a poetic rhyme.

(Note) I ain't got time to make every line rhyme,

Although rhyming some may be,

But this is truly an emergency.

Folks are starving and need to eat.

Some are homeless, begging,

And sleeping on the streets.

Crack has slithered in like a snake,

Eighteen rattles, and that ain't half the battle.

To God be the Glory

Murder is on the rampage,

There's cop killings and killer cops.

Black on Black crime is all too common (repeat)!

Black on Black crime all too common.

Yes, we needs to talk about that…

I ain't got time to make every line rhyme.

Mothers are crying, their children are dying.

They are falling like pecans from the tree

Stripped of all the goodies

And a shell is all you see.

We shouldn't be reading their obituary,

They shouldn't be over there in the cemetery;

Their full potentials had not been reached,

Yet some lie 6 feet deep.

I'm calling all you spitters and word go-getters,

The power of life and death lies in the tongue,

Uh-huh, the power of life and death lies in the tongue.

Let's use our vocals like wide open spickets,

Spewing out love and encouragement.

To God be the Glory

Let's show them and tell them that they are somebody.

They have purpose, hope, and a future.

Tell them all this killing one another

Is done unnecessarily and believe it or not

There are those who just sit back

And say the more the merrier.

Another one bites the dust,

Sad but I speak truth.

Again, calling all you spitters and word go-getter's.

Calling all you preachers and Sunday school teachers.

All you educators', motivators, and lawmakers.

Calling every race, age, culture, and gender.

We can and we must make a difference,

For this is truly an **EMERGENCY**.

Delores J. Gibson
The Barefooted Poet

<u>Apology</u>
By Delores Gibson

From ME to ME I deeply owe an apology.

I make no excuses for myself,

But I do apologize to myself

For listening to all those lies.

The "YOU ain't",

"YOU can't",

"YOU won't".

I apologize for giving room to the goal killers and the dream stealers.

Many precious years have gone bye;

I can't retrieve them no matter how I try,

But there's hope in knowing, I can regain

I do reclaim.

I will restore saith the lord, the years

That the canker worms, palmer worms, and caterpillars have eaten...

And they have been nibbling,

From ME to ME

I deeply owe an apology.

Delores J. Gibson
The Barefooted Poet

CHICKEN CHILE
By Delores Gibson

No alarm did rang, no song did sang, it was time to get up I knowed right after the rooster crowed. I'd yawn and stretch my legs, it was time to go out there and gather up them eggs

I'd go out in that chicken coop and there I'd step in all that chicken poop, you know I came to realize that made some of the best fertilizer.

I GUESS I'M JUST A CHICKEN CHILE.

My folk would rang that chicken neck, he would spitter and sputter, later that evening we had him on the table for supper.

They called me chicken too cause I wouldn't shoo the coo, but if my grandaddy had been your grandaddy you would've been chicken too

Now I got chickens on the wall, chickens down the hall, chicken at the windows, chicken at the door, even got chickens in the rug on the floor. I got a tick tock yep!! I got a chicken clock, I got chickens on the oven, chickens on the range, I even got a lil chicken change...

I GUESS I'M JUST A CHICKEN CHILE.

You can find chicken anywhere out there, there is chicken over rice, chicken done twice, chicken and tomatoes, chicken and potatoes. There's chicken tetrazzini and chicken Mazzolini. There's chicken and dressing, chicken can be quite a blessing...

You can find chicken anywhere out there... There's Hart's, Church's, Popeyes, Kentucky fried

Now necks and backs...I don't like that. Breast and wings, that's my thang...

I GUESS I'M JUST A CHICKEN CHILE

Delores J. Gibson
The Barefooted Poet

<u>Ms. Kiel</u>
By Delores Gibson

She was the teacher who believed in me, not because of beauty or brains.

I was just a plain ole Jane.

She told me to hold my head up high and walk with confidence

And to not let "can't" roll off my tongue.

She was tall, walked with her shoulders straight,

Strutted like a peacock, and she was pretty too.

She smelled like rose petals.

When she spoke, her voice was like calming thunder.

She made sense out of her every word.

She was fun, yet firm.

She was sassy, yet classy.

She had time for us all.

We all felt like we were her favorite,

BUT I KNEW DIFFERENT!

Delores J. Gibson
The Barefooted Poet

Just Another One
By Delores Gibson

What do you see when you look at another? Do you look with curious eyes, or do you look further? Do you look from within their heart, or do you simply choose to disregard? Well, what do you say when you see a troubled teen? Do you say that's not my daughter, that's not my son, that's just another one

Well, what crosses your mind when alcohol, cocaine, and crystal meth literally choke the life from some sister, brother, father, or mother? Do you hunch your shoulder and say, not my family, just some other?

How do you feel about the homelessness and hungriness that reaches our shore and in our world? Do you shake your head and say I feel sorry for that man, woman, boy, and girl.

Do you see and don't see

Do you hear and don't hear

Well, listen, what if GOD had said this about you and me while JESUS was stretched out on cavalry? What if he had said come, come down, MY SON. STOP. You're dying. He's not; she's not worthy; they just another one.

Instead, he turned his head while HIS SON suffered and bled and died, but I thank God he ROSE again for you and I and everyone.

Delores J. Gibson
The Barefooted Poet

Cassandra Sims Hansberrry

"Baby Girl"

Cassandra Sims Hansberry is a resident of Mobile, Alabama. She is a mother and grandmother currently working as an I.T. Systems Tech Sr. with the Alabama Department of Transportation. She enjoys helping others resolve problems and reach their goals. This position is perfect for her. It affords her the opportunity to help others by resolving their computer hardware and software related problems.

She's a member of Corpus Christi Catholic Church. In her spare time, she volunteers with Saint Vincent De Paul's Society to help raise funds and awareness for those most in need of resources to remain self-sufficient. She is also an avid volunteer with the American Cancer Society, working annually to raise funds and awareness for the South Alabama's Making Strides Against Breast Cancer Walk.

Her hobbies include daily walks, reading motivational and inspirational books, writing poetry and spending quality time with her grands. She is the founder of Heart and Soul Book Club. This book club was organized for its members to read and discuss motivational and inspirational books that motivates and inspires members to continuously develop in mind, body, heart and soul. It is also used as a platform for hosting positive life changing activities including poetry readings, dancercise, painting and self-love art projects.

Cassandra has been a member of Spoken Word of Mobile since 2016. It was one of the Monday night sessions she attended that reignited her interest in writing poetry. Her poem "Baby Girl" was one of her first poems written, after joining Spoken Word of Mobile.

Please Don't Pass Me By

By Cassandra Hansberry

My family brought me here to stay
Then they up and moved away
So when you walked through that door
My legs dropped to the floor.
I thought you were here for me
Sent by my family
I tried to stand in my head
But, nothing happened as my mind said
My heart jumped and skipped a beat
Because your coming here is a treat
I reached for you with my hand
But you did not understand
I wondered if you knew my name
Or wanted to play with me a board game
But, tears formed in my eye
As you began to pass me by
Again, I began to stair
As I sit here in this chair
I thought of when I was a little tike
And how I loved to ride my bike
And when I was a little girl
Singing and dancing while I twirled
And when I went off to college
It was to gain great knowledge
But, instead sealed my fate by getting married at 28
I thought of how I loved to run and once won a triathlon
I thought of how I like to eat more than I like this seat
I know my body is frail

But, I still have great stories to tell

So, please don't pass me by

Don't you see the tear in my eye?

My mind's still sharp

I'm not trying to harp

All I ask is that when you smile

Don't walk by me but sit a while

Let me tell you about my day

And how I came here to stay

Take the time to brush my hair

And help me with what to wear

Roll me up and down the hall

To keep me from staring at the wall

Take me outside the gate

And pretend we are on a date

And when you leave I will not cry

Because, you did not pass me bye.

©Cassandra Hansberry (June 2016)

When Life Takes A Loved One What Do You Do?
By Cassandra Hansberry

When life takes a loved one, you keep moving on
because your loved one is not really gone.

The physical body is not around so you won't hear them make a sound.
You won't be able to comb their hair or give them a loving stair.

There's no chance you will get a hug after the ground has been dug.
No, you won't be able to hold their hand as they walk through the Promised Land.

But you can feel them in your heart – their love for you will never part.
When you want to feel them there – be still and feel the air.

Talk to them from deep within and you will feel their love my friend.
Tell them how much you care – and you will feel their presence there.

The loss you feel won't subside but the love you feel will override.
So don't be scared, don't try to die, just know that God is awry.

He's not trying to hurt your heart or tear your family apart.
He just wants you to understand – that the power of life is in his hands.

We are never in control – life is his to have and to hold.
So dry your eyes and pray for peace, soon we will all be deceased.

©Cassandra Hansberry (September 2016)

Baby Girl
By Cassandra Hansberry

Little baby girl, cute as can be sitting over there watching me.
When I smile, when I frown, little baby girl puts it on.

Little baby girl, cute as can be sitting over there watching me.
When I cuss, when I fuss, little baby girl loses trust.

Little baby girl, cute as can be sitting over there watching me.
When I sing, when I dance, little baby girl learns about chance.

Little baby girl, cute as can be sitting over there watching me.
When I read, when I write little baby girl gains the light.

Little baby girl, cute as can be sitting over there watching me.
When I am lit and unfit little baby girl begins to quit.

Little baby girl, cute as can be sitting over there watching me.
When I kill, when I steal little baby girl feels surreal.

Little baby girl, cute as can be sitting over there watching me.
When I'm hit, when I fight, little baby girl is filled with fright.

Little baby girl, cute as can be sitting over there watching me.
When I dope, when I smoke little baby girl cannot cope.

Little baby girl, cute as can be sitting over there watching me.
When I scream, when I shout, little baby girl begins to doubt.

Little baby girl, cute as can be sitting over there watching me.
When I am angry, when I am mad, little baby girl feels sad.

Little baby girl, cute as can be sitting over there watching me.
When I pray, and show love, little baby girl is as free as a dove.

Little baby girl, cute as can be sitting over there modeling me.

©Cassandra Hansberry (September 16, 2016)

LaMya Hatton

LaMya Hatton was born in Mobile Alabama on October 15, 2005 to the parents of Stephanie Arnold and Carvenus Hatton. She is an inspiring young high school junior who is 17 years old. She is an only child so she gets a lot of thinking and contemplating time to herself.

What inspired her to write poetry was her wanting to let out her feelings and become a better writer. Drawing was a form of an outlet for her. But over the years, it was starting to not be enough because of her depression and no motivation.

In English class, whenever they read poetry, She would always be inspired by how poetry can flow so smoothly and she was interested in how people formed their words so smartly. How people were able to rhyme in poetry always fascinated her and she wanted to try writing her own poems because she thought it would make her seem more intelligent and creative.

Around the 7th grade, she started trying to write her own poetry. But she didn't know how to really form a poem, so she just kind of stopped. It wasn't until high school, in the 10th grade, when she started back to writing again. Her Creative Writing teacher inspired her but she felt discouraged because whenever they had to write their own poems, she felt like her poems weren't good enough.

When she got to the 11th grade she joined the Optimist Boys and Girls Club. She enjoys going there because of the opportunities. One day, they had a special event at the Club involving poetry. She decided to join this event. When she read her poem to one of the staff, she saw a certain potential in her and asked her to join Spoken Word at Toulminville Library. She was nervous to go because she already knew everyone there would have great poems, except her. But when she got there and actually read her poetry, they liked it. They wanted her to join them more often. They also introduced her to poetry opportunities outside of Spoken Word. It made her really happy and feel proud of herself. So this place became her outlet as well as poetry. So, now she has poetry as a new hobby and it has inspired her to become a writer and practice writing more about how she feels and other things too.

....

Thank you Spoken Word and everyone else who has helped me reach this point in my creative journey.

Cost of Violence
By LaMya Hatton

A gun
Used for no good
Sometimes used to shoot all throughout neighborhoods
Somehow kids get a hold of them
Shooting up nearby schools
If not killing each other, it's killing themselves
Mental health so bad, you can't help them because it's already too late
They're swallowed up by sadness and hate
Hate for no reason
Sadness caused by trauma
These adults ain't no help
Preaching to kids to be gangster
Preaching to young boys to be tough and be a man
They don't even realize that's a five year boy
Now kids runnin' on streets
Not even realizing the cops are watchin'
Ready to shoot you because you a black child with a deadly weapon
These kids don't realize the reality
These white folks out here don't care about your mentality
With that deadly gun they see you as a criminal
They already ready to call you out a killer
They already ready to put in jail behind a cell for the rest of your life
Don't go wondering, "what happened to my life?"
Because what happened was you picked up that gun and you chose to fight

-    **LaMya Hatton**

Honor For Our People
By LaMya Hatton

Education is something that we as black people

Should value because our ancestors

Have fought very hard for us

To be educated and educated properly

And to just say that we do not want to learn

Is throwing away all of that hard work.

So by getting an education

And doing something with the knowledge

That we have gained from it

Is showing appreciation

To our ancestors and honoring them.

- **LaMya Hatton**

Take A Stand
By LaMya Hatton

We are given opportunities as a new generation. We don't take advantage of these opportunities at all. Our ancestors were never given these chances we now have. And when we waste our time and days away, it's disappointing to the ones who fought and worked so hard to get us to where we are. And when we slack off, goof off, fight, and act like fools it shows others that we don't have appreciation for what we have and what was given to us. Not only that, it makes society think that all the stereotypes about us are true. It's up to us to not only continue to make a change, but to make a change within ourselves. So we must fill our minds with knowledge and educate ourselves and each other to adapt, grow, and build our own, take care of our own, hold our own, and help our own. And it won't just be to prove and show society that it's wrong about us, but it'll be to help ourselves and our own community. Because we have the power, mindset, and will to do these things if we only try.

- **LaMya Hatton**

Violence Is Weak
By LaMya Hatton

When I think violence

I think cowardice

People who don't know how to put up a peaceful

fight

They use fists

They use knives

They use guns They use tanks

They use war

And then call themselves strong and gangster

For killing a man instead walking away

What a weak way

To express what you could've just said A simple situation

Turned into a violent altercation

Now a man rots

When all it took was a peaceful talk

-   **LaMya Hatton**

Visions of Blackness
By LaMya Hatton

When you see black, what do you see?

Do you see youth?

Do you see beauty?

Do you think free?

Do you see someone who knows how to be a king or queen?

And if you do, how does black carry on in your visions?

Does black wear their natural, big, curly crowns? Or does black preach freedom and fight for their rights?

Does black dance the dance of life?

Does black's complexion glimmer in the day and night?

Does black's aura come off as beautiful?

Or does it come off as royal?

Does black never show not a single wrinkle in their skin?

Does black make you want to be beautiful

To be royal

To be free

To be youthful?

Because all of those things are black to me

And black is all I'll ever want to be

- **LaMya Hatton**

Feelings Are Strange
By LaMya Hatton

Feelings are strange

Feelings can range

Feelings can swing

High or low

They can make you want to drop to the floor

Or just make you wanna drop dead

Feelings are strange

Feelings are deep

Deep as the ocean

Swimming not knowing their direction

Whether they should float, go, or stay

Feelings are strange

Feelings can be the best

Or be just the worse

They can be nice

Or they can be mean

They can be keen

Or they can be blunt

Feelings are strange

You never know

They disappear

Like a mosquito

A hidden nuisance

That you can't get rid of

Feelings are strange When they hide

They hide well

Stayed put as you dwell

For a long time, no tell

Or they can be long forgotten

Only to be broughten

When reminded of something known long

Ago and all too well

Feelings are strange

They are misunderstood

Like that one kid in class You never really knew existed Until you meet them

And realize too

That they are misunderstood just like you

Feelings are strange

Feelings are sometimes not wanted

Although sometimes needed

To express what we what we can't explain

They should be expressed calmly

So we can all live in harmony

Feelings are strange

They can hurt like a punch

Or feel good like a soft touch

Some say they feel like a still tree

While others claim they feel like a hollow shell

Feelings are strange

They make you do different things

Like love and fall in love

Or hate and destroy

Feelings are strange

We all feel them in different ways

We all just have to make sure that we know they matter

Whether big or small

Complicated or easy

They all come by to us with no reason

Maybe a visit

Maybe a stay

We just have to be considerate of other people's feelings and take care of our own

Because at the end of the day

We all have strange feelings

Some that are very revealing

Some we don't want to stay

Those are the feelings we tuck

We tuck away

- **LaMya Hatton**

<u>Rise</u>
By LaMya Hatton

Black child, rise

It's time to now take pride

It's time to strive

It's now time to take stride

Black child, rise

And look upon the path before you

Will you walk

Or will you fly

Black child, rise

It's time to make a change

Either within yourself

The community

Or the world

Black child, rise

Quit mopin'

Because the world don't owe you nothing

If you want the world to see your worth

You got to show them what you got to offer

Black child, rise

It's time to start working hard

Quit foolin' around with those losers that don't do

nothing but sit on they behind

Laziness don't get you nowhere

Black child, rise

It's time to find your destiny

Don't pay attention to them

They don't see your potential

Black child you have a brightness in you that needs to shine.

Whether you know it or not. Don't let it go to waste.

Don't listen to all that noise and don't ever give up.

There's something in you that would surely make people look up to you.

- **LaMya Hatton**

Marlette Holt

"Journey"

Marlette "Journey" Holt is a mother, a minister, an author, a playwright, a YouTuber and lover of all things positive. Marlette has dedicated her life to the service of God's people by encouraging and enlightening through the beautiful use of words. The realization that words are spirits prompted Marlette to not only minister through poetry, but to also start her own YouTube channel "Marley's Chronicles" which encourages self-evolution by facing and overcoming childhood traumas. In addition to poetry, writing books and YouTubing, Marlette "Journey" Holt has written and acted in many plays. Some can be found on the YouTube channel "Beatrice Theatrics".

God has given us all many ways to serve each other, Marlette "Journey" Holt has used her love of words to be a blessing to many.

The Treasure Hunt
By Marlette "Journey" Holt

How do you light the fire that so patiently waits below?

How do you stir the embers of your passion?

The passion that sits in your bowels and screams,

"I'm here, let me go!"

How do you ignite the sparks of life

That have been quenched with disappoints, failures and fears?

How do you let loose the overwhelming burning desires

That have been blanketed by years and years of tears?

Do you pray? Do you wait? Do you hope? Do you dream?

What do you do with the seed that's been planted so deep within? What do you do with

the thoughts of happiness and success

That shows his face every now and again?

What do you do with the love

That nudges you to go forward, to move ahead?

What do you do with the soft quiet voice that whispers in your ear,

"Go on girl, you're not dead!"?

Do you pray? Do you wait? Do you hope? Do you dream?

No my friend, too much of that has already been done!

Open your eyes and realize, it's you! You are the one!

So you walk, and walk, and walk some more.

With your head held high and your shoulders in place

You say to yourself, "this is who I am,

I'm not in a race"

And when you come to yourself, you will realize

That your embers have been sparked, and your sparks have become flames

And your flames have burst into a wildfire of fulfillment, joy, happiness and pleasure

It's all waiting on you, your Indwelled Treasures.

\-   ***Marlette "Journey" Holt***

I Am Journey
By Marlette "Journey" Holt

Yes, I am Journey

What you see is not what I have been, nor is it what I shall be But it's a glimpse of my

travels with truth mingled with the twists and turns From where my life has brought me.

I am Journey

I am neither here nor there

But a continual movement of practical experiences

In which poetry allows me to share.

My sisters and brothers

Do not be dismayed of the image you see

For I am still on my Path,

I am Journey, headed for my destiny.

- *Marlette "Journey" Holt*

My Employer
By Marlette "Journey" Holt

I have the best job in the world!

With the world's greatest employer.

My employer has connections all over the world. He knows every judge on every continent. There is nowhere on the Earth that my employer doesn't have the hook up. Honey! He has more money than Bill Gates, Donald Trump and Oprah put together and multiplied! He loves to share.

When I complete my tasks, he gives me special rewards.

And benefits! What! I don't even need health insurance because my employer gives me good health. 401K, savings, retirement! Man, I've got the best retirement plan there is as long as I continue to work for him. When I retire, not only will I have my own personal mansion, but it will be on a street paved with gold. My employer is the best!

He has an open-door policy too.

When I have personal problems with children or bills or whatever, I'll go to my employer to talk about time off so I can handle it, do you know what my employer says?

He says, "Do you love your job?"

I say, "Yes sir"

He says, 'Do you really want to stop doing what you're doing?"

I say, "No sir"

He says, "Continue to work, I'll fix it for you"

I say, "Thank you sir!"

My employer is the best!

You know, my employer once sacrificed his only son to make sure everybody had a chance to work for him. My employer is everywhere, all the time at any given time.

My employer is so powerful, that he can speak and things change. He can blow his breath and things come alive. He could bat his eye and the whole world would crumble!

My employer is the best!

You may have heard of him. Some people call him Jehovah-jireh, because he always provides for them. Or they may call him a Wonderful Counselor, because he gives the best advice with the best results. Or they may even call him the Rose of Sharon because he is beauty in dark and dry places.

But I simply call my employer Mr. I Am, because he is EVERYTHING I need him to be.

Wow! My employer, He's the best!

- *Marlette "Journey" Holt*

Beverly Jo Jones

Beverly Jo Jones is a member of Spoken Word of Mobile that meets at the Toulminville branch of the Mobile Public Library. All her life, she has lived in Alabama--Robertsdale in childhood, Mobile County since then except two years in Gadsden. She completed Citronelle High School, Faulkner Junior College, Bay Minette, (A.A.) and Anthem Online College, Arizona (A.S.and one year to B.S) For this anthology, she offers one poem read to the poets since 2006, and four read since 2011. Some of her poems are own personal insights set to old rhythms or poetry meter.

Except for a few poems required in school days, her lyrics are sparked by historical and current events--constitutional rights as "Ode to Roy S. Moore" and "A Memorial to R.F.K"; history in "Peter Pilgrim" who discovered the English had the first Thanksgiving before the Pilgrims; current events as "Oh, Oh, Oh Searcy", "Nobody Loves You" (except reporters) and "The Iron Bowl..2017" and "...2019"; prison humor as in "Sweat, But Not the Small Stuff" and "Attorney General vs Tobacco Users in Prison"; family topics as "Come Back to Erin, Savannah" (the dachshund's running away from home likened to the Southern States trying to withdraw from The Union), "My Mama's Daddy Was A Cobbler" and many others.

Oh, Searcy, (Sir, See!)
By Beverly Jo Jones

Oh, oh, oh Searcy, dearest ole Searcy,

You're the gathering place for all who are unique.

When the___the Judge sees beautiful Searcy,

From the inside out, he'll never more want to peek!

Dearest Sir, See! Come in and see Searcy.

A commitment from the Judge will get you in.

Oh! So elating! And oh so dismaying!

You will fight for human rights from now to birth's end.

Quite the historic fort it once kept here,

Ole Geronimo would do and dare to flight.

Lurleen Wallace hangs in the foyer.

Comes soon, her hope and prayer for e__e__e__equal rights.

Oh, oh, oh Sir See, come in and see Searcy.

The canteen is the central meeting place.

If the d____d___doctors and the d___d___degreed ones

Left, the halls, walls and grounds of Searcy would be safe.

- **Copyrights Beverly Jo Jones...July 8, 2002**

Ode to Troy, the King, Alabama Attorney General

vs. Tobacco Users in Prison

vs. British Petroleum Oil

By Beverly Jo Jones

Pardon me, please!

This air is to breathe,

Not yours to pollute

'Les you want lawsuits.

Therefore, best get you wise.

Stop your crummy, scummy cries,

Or you will be like BP with Troy, the King

Cutting your tails before Spring.

Just wait till you see Federal sanctions!

You'll wish you'd taken more firm action

To curb your tobacco appetite

By doing your loitering time

In *Physical Education* Exercise.

Troy is no commoners name

Whereby, Alabama is not in a *Trojan Horse* game.

When it elected the Attorney General

It was not to protect criminals.

-   **By Beverly Jo Jones (2010)**

Sweat! But not the Small Stuff
By Beverly Jo Jones

Don't sweat the small stuff

Is an axiom, maxim, adage to say.

Here we are: Using state money to pay

Grown fellows and ladies to huff and puff

Over whether or not convicts got all the dust up or not.

I say! Let the wind blow it away

And save tax dollars to play,

Exercise, badminton, tennis or croquet.

Dismiss huffy, puffy small-stuff staff.

Let them find a real JOB in Eskimo igloo land

Sweating in search of gold dust.

- **by Beverly Jo Jones (© 2010)**

My Mama's Daddy was a Cobbler
By Beverly Jo Jones

I don't plan to grow old like you plan,

So don't set me to your dull daze.

I have and had goals fortuitous

That requires my stage never fade.

So get out of my way hags and warlocks,

And go mend your old shoddy, foddy shoes.

You can't, you know.

Ha Ha Ha Ha Ha, because

Your plastic holds neither needle nor thread

  Nor tack, nor shoe-button,

But my leather-made shoes do.

by Beverly Jo Jones (© 2010)

Come Back to *Erin, Savannah, Savannah*
By Beverly Jo Jones

Note: To melody & rhyme of "Come Back to Erin, Mavoureen, Mavoureen"

Come back to *Erin, Savannah, Savannah*.

Please do return NOW

Your dog tags are here (home in Saraland, AL 36571)

Ye shall not go out

A roamin' away for

Ye shall su. re... ly

Find no food, free.

Oh, Dear, *Savannah*!

Your leaving despairs ALL.

Must you pretend you're so Brave?

While you aren't?

Come back to *Erin, Savannah, Savannah*.

Dog Catchers in Saraland

Will find and lock you up.

Dear Me, *Savannah,* it's costly to free thee.

Dog Pounds aren't free, they charge high to free, thee.

Cost of your upkeep

Is high enough at your own home.

Why you'd expect us

To pay a Dog Pound

Lacks Dog sense.

Come Back to *Erin, Savannah, Savannah*,

Daddy might spank you for leaving the Yard,

Mother will certainly leash you for life, Now!

Oh, Dear *Savannah*, See Now, your Wanting to Roam Free is Anti-Dog Laws.

Dogs have no Civil Rights, *Savannah* -- Stay Home Now!

- **Beverly Jo Jones © BJJ 2013**

Cheryl "CJ" Jones

My name is Cheryl Jones, aka poet cj and I was born in Mobile, Alabama, raised in Philadelphia, Pennsylvania for the majority of my life with visits every summer and throughout the year back to Mobile, Alabama and Jackson, Mississippi where my grandparents lived. After graduating from Temple University in 1997, I purchased a one-way ticket and relocated back to Mobile, Alabama in August 1998 to get a sense of home that I had never experienced and to attend graduate school at Alabama State University. As a person in a foreign land, I began to slowly make my way through town and found many awesome possibilities. 'Jazzy Blues Café' was about to open, 'Jazz Street' shortly thereafter opened up and poetry flowed from me in both establishments on a weekly basis. Things happened where 'Gulf Coast Ethnic and Heritage Festival' took off and I wanted to be a part of the greatness. One day, it happened, I was asked to be a part of the Board and accepted with honor. As the poet of the group, I was charged with finding a location for the upcoming jazz show featuring and a night of poetry. In searching for a location I came across the 'Toulminville Branch Library' and in looking it over realized it wasn't large enough for the expected crowd. As a result, I began filling out an application for myself and when Ms. Gertrude Lafitte asked me the name of the group I simply shared I didn't have a name; however, would come up with something upon completing the application. And there it was born, 'Spoken Word of Mobile' in April 2001.

When I write, it is a freeing release of everything inside of me. As technology has been a more precise way of me getting all of myself out, I record my words and then transcribe them into writings of all sorts. Poetry is a bag I have been carrying for a lifetime and I didn't really realize it until I relocated back to Mobile in 1998. The inspirations of my poetic expressions have always come from within myself by way of experiences of my own and those of others, things I see and hear about in passing throughout my day, my emotions of sorts, issues happening in the world, and so many other topics that can come to mind. The podium that I opened up for all to come and be free too is 'Spoken Word of Mobile' a place that holds love, peace, prosperity and poetry to any and all that have come through the threshold of the space.

- **Cheryl "CJ" Jones**

American Heroes
By cj

Today our American Heroes come in many different ways of volunteers, professions, ethnicities and religious backgrounds, and genders

American Heroes come in different ways in the form of volunteers

Volunteers help so many people each and every day

Volunteers are regular every day people who may or may not be highly trained to help so many people to get back on track and survive in many trying situations and circumstances

Volunteers can be you and me to help so many people to see life in a better and more positive light

Volunteers are blessings from god

American Heroes come in many different professions of dedicated people

Professions of dedicated people help so many people each and every day

Professions of dedicated people like the American Red Cross workers, social workers, firefighters, police officers, doctors, nurses, educators, the media arena, delivery service individuals, postal workers, farmers, chefs, entrepreneurs, fundraisers, and all essential workers of all sorts help so many people to get back on track and survive in many trying situations and circumstances

Professions of dedicated people help other people to find hope, love, joy, and the possibilities of going on although things will not be the same and that they can prosper and help so many people to see life in a better and more positive light

Professions of dedicated people are blessing from god

American Heroes come in many different ethnicities and religious backgrounds

Ethnicities and religious backgrounds can help so many people each and every day

Ethnicities and religious backgrounds create a world of diversity which we call a melting pot which allows so many people to get back on track and survive in many trying situations and circumstances

Ethnicities and religious backgrounds allow one to feel comfortable seeing someone like them in order to understand through language barriers, cultures, and the like to help so many people to see life in a better and more positive light

Ethnicities and religious backgrounds are blessing from god

American Heroes come in female and male genders

Women and men help so many people each and every day

Women and men can exert their expertise and talents in the environment in which they are in to help so many people to get back on track and survive in many trying situations and circumstances

Women and men together can rebuild marriages, communities, interdependence, dreams, family connections, goals, relationships, and whatever one's heart desires and needs to help so many people to see life in a better and more positive light

Women and men are blessings from god

Today our American Heroes come in many different ways of volunteers, professions, ethnicities and religious backgrounds, and genders

Today take time out of your life to become an American Hero, if not for yourself, then for someone else and remember that you to are a blessing from god!

- **cj**

Happiness
By cj

Throughout my life, happiness is something that I always felt the need to be in search of, or was it something that my parents talked about because they were in search of this thing called happiness

As my life progressed, I began to realize that happiness is not something you talk about, for it is an inner sense of self and the joy in which one exerts and lives in

Happiness is not tangible!
Happiness is not inherited!
Happiness is not always all day, everyday!

In today's world, many people talk about being happy and/or the happiness in which they feel

What exactly is happiness? And if happiness is what one possesses, then why is today's world so messed up?

In this world, our place called life, we tend to misguide and misrepresent what happiness is all about and what it looks like

Happiness is not found when seeking it in someone else!!
Happiness is not all the money in the world!!
Happiness is not having it done our way all the time!!

At this juncture of life's game, happiness is definitely something that we all have to work at in order to accomplish it and maintain it

As some of you have experienced life's disappointments that can cause one to lose sight of happiness

Just when you thought you fell out the happiness zone, you wake up and realize that your happiness is a lot more worthwhile than any disappointment

Happiness is having faith in the Mother Father Lord God!!!
Happiness is who you are!!!
Happiness is always a part of self!!!

So, the next time you feel that a search for happiness needs to take effect or you hear or see someone lacking happiness, remind yourself and them, that although happiness seems so far out of reach, just look inside of yourself and realize that you are your own happiness and it already lies within you

Happiness is here and now!!!!
Happiness is you and me!!!!
Happiness is forever!!!!

-    **cj**

Radical
By cj

when i speak my mind,
    you wanna call me radical

when i do things my way,
    you wanna call me radical

when i choose not to play the game,
    you wanna call me radical

when i don't use the terms 'yes sir' and 'no ma'am,'
    you wanna call me radical

when i create my own employment,
    you wanna call me radical

when i empower myself,
    you wanna call me radical

when i make things happen,
    you wanna call me radical

when i communicate my reality,
    you wanna call me radical

when i share information,
    you wanna call me radical

when i show care and concern for my people,
    you wanna call me radical

when i fight for myself,
    you wanna call me radical

when i have my own identify,
    you wanna call me radical

when i exceed the norm,
    you wanna call me radical

when i know who I am,
    you wanna call me radical

when i know where i have come from,
　　　you wanna call me radical

when i know where i am going,
　　　you wanna call me radical

now i know that you divided my world
now i know that you know all that I possess
now i know that you caused much remorse and pain
now i know that you set out to destroy my people
now i know that you burned my house of worship
now i know that you continuously keep my people down
now i know that you inport the guns and drugs
now i know that you are jealous of me
now i know that you choose not to understand
now i know that you conquered and divided my family
now i know that you stole my identify
now i now that you played a big role in who my people are today
now i know that you hate my existence
now i know that you no longer have any use for me
now i know that you know that time it really is
now i know that you soon will be in the minority
you wanna call me RADICAL ---
--- I ACCEPT!

sistahs & brothahs… once you know, you cannot go back to not knowing

-    **cj**

A Relationship is the Giving of Oneself
By cj

A relationship is the giving of oneself,

some ingredients are communicating, uplifting, loving, compromising and sharing.

No matter whom you are in a relationship with,

mother, father, sister, brother, husband, wife, lover, friend, co-worker and/or children

A relationship is the giving of oneself.

In a relationship, we must understand that without communication,

how can two people challenge, get to know each other and achieve goals?

In a relationship, we must understand that without upliftment,

how can two people elevate conductively, be appreciative of each other and achieve goals?

In a relationship, we must understand that without love,

how can two people grow, survive tribulations and achieve goals?

In a relationship, we must understand that without compromise,

how can two people learn from each other, obtain discipline and achieve goals?

In a relationship, we must understand that without sharing,

how can two people establish a strong bond, receive from each other and achieve goals?

A relationship is the giving of oneself.

Brothers, learn to empower your sisters so that the can become great mothers, lovers and powerful women with uplifting spirits and confidence living in this world full of turmoil and challenge.

Sisters, learn to empower your brothers so that the can become great husbands, leaders, and men of surviving spirits and egos living in this world full of trial and tribulation.

Brothers and sisters, we must learn to give of ourselves so we can acquire the tools of wisdom, accomplishment, peace and most of all what GOD has planned for our lives

A relationship is the giving of oneself.

Love yourselves first so that you can love others.

Forgive yourselves first so that you can forgive others.

Enjoy yourselves first so that you can enjoy others.

Empower yourselves first so that you can empower others.

A relationship is the giving of oneself.

- **cj**

Sunday
By cj

A day to really worship and show the LORD how much you love HIM

A day to accept the LORD's supper to regenerate the faith and peace that you always carry in your soul

A day to thank the Mother Father LORD GOD for all your blessings this past week and for the week ahead

A day to pay tithes to let GOD know HE is who provided

A day to thank our ancestors for all that they give

A day to learn Sunday School education

A day to listen to gospel music and inspirational music

A day to celebrate the start of a new week

A day to prepare for the next five days

A day to take a long stroll after dinner

A day to bake cookies, breads, and cakes

A day to walk three miles to get your workout schedule started

A day to get your coils retwisted so the hair can loc

A day to cook a large meal for yourself and/or your family and friends

A day to watch all the children do what you would have usually done

A day to spend time with your mate and make love

A day to soak in the bathtub with candles and incense

A day to tell someone that you love them

A day to know who you are and determine how you are standing

A day to love yourself

A day to finish up any lingering homework that needs completion

A day to study for the upcoming test in Life 101

A day to slow down and meditate on last week's challenges

A day to make your long distance phone calls

A day to balance your checkbook

A day to go shopping in New York City's Greenwich Village and SOHO

A day to visit the museum

A day to hang out with a friend

A day to travel back home when out of town

A day to go to a jazz club for a glass of Merlot and live entertainment

A day to catch up on pre-recorded soap operas that during the week there is no time to view

A day to catch that long overdue movie

A day before a holiday or rather an excuse not to work on Monday

A day to spring forward or fall back in time

A day to set aside for many preparations

- **cj**

What Time Is It?
By cj

blossoming and flowing into the world that for all your life you had been told about, for all your life you have been sheltered from...

> ...What Time Is It?

seeing the opportunities and hearing the cries of my people who cannot get a decent pay and benefit packaged job...

> ...What Time Is It?

sisters and brothers for whatever our reasons, seem to want the struggle and ongoing confusion instead of simply coming and getting together for the sake of loving each other...

> ...What Time Is It?

families lacking loyalties, honesty, and trusting relationships within their own gang which helps to contribute to the dysfunction in our schools today...

...What Time Is It?
What Time Is It?
What Time Is It?

it is time for our people to tell the truth to our children and let them know what the world is about and what it can offer so that they can blossom and flow with confidence and self-worth...

> ...What Time Is It?

it is time for our people to obtain opportunity in all its variations and accept all the responsibilities that come along with it so that our cries can become laughter and smiles...
> ...What Time Is It?

it is time for our people to stop being messy with the piles and trials of ongoing experiences. we must begin to mature and grow as a people in order to cease struggle and confusion, in order to love each other. brothers and sisters, be open to change and challenge so that we can begin to love each other again...

...What Time Is It?

it is time for our people to regain what our family structure has lost--honor, dignity, and respect. without these three elements, our children will not be loyal, honest, or trusting to themselves, let alone their families, teachers, and peers. teach self-love so that families can seek structure in our future…

…What Time Is It?

it is the 21st century and time is getting shorter for our people and the greater future of our people

it is the 21st century and we still have a lot to overcome

it is the 21st century and one day soon we will all wake up and know exactly What Time It Is!

are you awake?
what time do you have?
wake up and tell me,

What Time Is It?

- **cj**

Gert Laffiette

"Peace Maker"

Gertrude Clark Laffiette is a wife, mother and grandmother who as of this writing has been employed by Mobile Public Library for 47 years; she has been the liaison and a member of Spoken Word of Mobile from its beginning. Her poet's name is "Peace maker;" because by the grace and power of God she has the uncanny ability to promote peace in the midst of turmoil. Her prayers are to embody fearless patience, love, and the understanding to know when confrontation is necessary but in all things promote God's love through peaceful means.

Peace Maker was a lover of Words From early childhood. The only books that were available to her in her home environment as an adolescent was a dictionary and a set of encyclopedias which she read from cover to cover.

Peace Maker is excited and grateful to Willie Dinish, Black Ink Coalition for sharing his time, gifts and talents with the group and for allowing the Spoken Word of Mobile the possibility of putting together an anthology of poetry. It is an honor and a privilege to be affiliated with this group of people; Spoken Word of Mobile. The words that live within this book will change lives..

Just Like a Rose
By **Gert Laffiette**

Like a rose, you are treasured

A precious GEM from Above;

Created from the depths

Of God's amazing love.

Like a ROSE you are delicate

So special to the touch;

Always remember that

You are loved so very much.

Like a ROSE you are special

Nothing else can compare;

You're accepted and protected

In God's divine care.

Like a ROSE you are beautiful

A bright and shining star;

Please believe me when I tell you,

That a ROSE is what you are.

- **Gert Laffiette**

Love and Marriage
By Gert Laffiette

Love and Marriage

It is not always easy; but it is worth it.

I am bone of his bone;

And flesh of his flesh.

God laid him down;

And took me from his chest.

With his eyes he told me;

That I had captured his heart.

God gave me the power to do that part.

God said he'd leave his parents

And cleave to his wife.

Now, I'm his Queen in Love;

And he's my King for life.

No; marriage has not been a flowered bed of ease;

It has taken God, patience and much love to please.

The Song of Solomon says it best; grab the Bible and you can read the rest.

** "I am his and he is mine."

We're like fine wine, we get better and better with time.

- **Gert Laffiette**

(Song of Solomon 6:3) Dedicated to the love of my Life: My husband J.P.

Let's Rock the Word
By Gert Laffiette

We're here today to celebrate;

Our freedom to communicate.

To share the word and meditate

Let's ROCK THE WORD!

Let's ROCK THE WORD!

Let's shed some light – illuminate

and let's be clear – enunciate

Let's ROCK THE WORD!

Let's ROCK THE WORD!

Let's search and seek – Investigate

We can use the word to - Medicate

With the Spoken Word we can dedicate

Encourage others to participate

Let's do it now; don't need to wait.

We've got to learn to appreciate.

The Power of God's Spoken Word

Let's Rock the WORD because the WORD Rocks The WORLD!

"Your word is a lamp to my feet and a light to my path." Psalm 119:105

"All Scripture is breathed out by God and profitable for teaching, for reproof, for correction, and for training in righteousness." 2 Timothy 3:16

And we also thank God continually because, when you received the word of God, which you heard from us, you accepted it not as a human word, but as it actually is, the word of God, which is indeed at work in you who believe. 1 Thessalonians 2:13

- **Gert Laffiette**

So Full of Joy
By Gert Laffiette

Today I am so full of Joy
You've entrusted me with this baby boy.

Because you have, I promise you;
I'll guard his life, my whole life through.

TODAY, I AM SO FULL OF JOY

Today, to you I lift up his life;
From your holy word, I'll take advice.

I give him back to you today;
To serve you in a perfect way.

TODAY I AM SO FULL OF JOY

Who am I that you consider me?
Help me God, to honor thee.

For "this man-child that you have made,
To love and honor you to him I'll persuade.

TODAY I AM SO FULL OF JOY

Feel free to use him for your glory,

Make him a part of your holy story;

Finally, I say Thank you God

- **Gert Laffiette**

Dedicated to Cassandra Sims and her blessed Bundle of Joy. May he one day change the world for God.

Wanda R. Seals Lewis

Wanda Lewis is a native of Mobile AL and Gilbertown AL. She is the wife of Garfield Lewis, and mother of two adult children, Shanthalitta Wallace and James Seals IV. She is also the proud grandmother of two granddaughters, Nadya Maiben and TaMiyah Seals.

She and her husband, Garfield perform as "Words and Melody" a poetic and a cappella duo. They both are members of Spoken word of Mobile. Their goal is to assist in educating the community through words and song, they both love to garden and perform as much as possible.

Wanda is the author of several self-published books, Expressions Through Experiences, a collection of poetry, Every Soul has a Story, A collection of short stories, poetry and meditations. A Balanced Body, a health guide, for mind, body and spirit. She has one CD project Smoothetry, poetry set to smooth jazz. Contact information: wandalewis1005@gmail.com

154

Shine On
By Wanda Lewis

Don't be afraid to stand up for what you believe in

If War is wrong, make a stand!

Stand up for what is right

Steadfast don't give up the fight

The forces are with you, strength, courage, wisdom and mercy

Our rights are slowly being taken away, can't you see?

There is a season for everything

This is the season to let freedom ring

Shine on bright star

The path is dim but the light is bright

Change the world, with your words and songs

This is our world and we all belong

Shine on, Shine on

By: Wanda R. Seals Lewis

The Hat Lady
By Wanda Lewis

As she walks down the street

Matching from head to toe and always neat

Her purse, shoes, scarf, gloves and of course hat to match

Most guys would say "hmm what a good catch"

Hats of many colors and unique designs she will blow your mind

Come here chile let me take you to a different point in time

Back in the day round the 1800's we didn't have no hat to were on our heads

We only had rags that we tore from strips of cloth that covered our beds

We watched the white women in their fine hats prancing around town

They had all kind of hats, hats with feathers, ribbons, lace and some leather bound

They loved those hats and wanted some to shade and adorn their beautiful heads

They wanted hats for worship, hats for play, hats for work and hats when they wed

After all was said they began to get educated, learning to read by candle light

With those fancy hats in their sights, they worked from morning to night

They saved every penny they could rake or scrape and bought all kinds of hats

Honey chile those cats went wild with those hats

They bought fancy hats, jazzy hats, casual hats, hats with brims

Hats with flowers, hats with straw, and hats with golden rims

So now when you put your hat on your head and take a twirl,

Remember that rags once adorned the heads of our ancestors in this world

Thank God for the journey and the victory and the story the hat tells

We celebrate today strength, and wisdom

and we stand on the shoulders of the Women

Who were the first Hat Ladies.

By: Wanda S. Lewis

My Flowers
By Wanda Lewis

Please don't give me my flowers while I lay

Stretched out in my grave

Give them to me while I can

Smell them and appreciate

The sweet aroma they make

then I can give you back a wave

A thank you

And a how do you do?

I love the majestic smell

Floating through the air

It lets me know all is well with me

I love to feel the dampness of the pedals

Resting against my cheeks

The splendor my eyes, venture to seek

So, just give me my flowers while I can still breathe

And not the one bereaved!

By: Wanda S. Lewis

Who was U.S. President Then?
By Wanda Lewis

A Tribute to 100 years with Theresa Frost & Arnesa Sole

The year was 1919 the month was March,

twin baby girls came into this world.

One name Theresa the other one Arnesa

Can I get an amen?

Who was the President then?

Woodrow Wilson (1913-1921)

They grew to be two cute girls now about four.

They were smart as a whip and looked just alike

Yet one was Puddin and the other one Spice

Saddie was sassy and spoke her mind

Puddin is quiet and let's her sweetness shine

Who is the President that comes to mind

At this point in time?

Warren Harding (1921-1923)

This dynamic duo is now about eight years old.

Listening to ragtime music and good ole soul.

Walking to school down dusty dirt roads

Sometimes carrying heavy loads

Schooling was important even way back then

Wonder who was the President way back when.
Calvin Coolidge (1923-1929)

Time flew by, they are now around twelve years old
Pretty but not proper, they had to work in the fields picking cotton
They kept the faith, and prayed daily that one day things wouldn't be so rotten

Too the Sisters life really did stink
Who was the President then you think?
Hubert Hoover (1929-1933)

How time has passed, they are around sixteen years old
Old enough to work in the big house, cooking and cleaning
and taking care of kids was not demeaning
they did their job and they did it well
So well, until they became a part of the family for whom they cared.

So do tell, now who do you think was President during this spell?
Franklin D. Roosevelt (1933-1945)

They are grown now, twenty years plus, white people running for election
The country in need of a resurrection
Blacks denied the right to vote, hard times and battles to win

Who do you think was the President back then?
Harry S. Truman (1945-1954)

Now both in their late twenties, both grown, married and with children

Theresa married Daniel frost and begot Lucinda and James

Arnesa married Lenard Sole, they begot Theresa, (Arnesa (Ann) and Anthony)

Black families back in the day, struggling to make it, trying to keep it legit

Who was the President? Was his eyes open or did he just sit?

Dwight Eisenhower (1953-1961)

They are now in their roaring thirties,

hard working women teaching life lessons.

For each generation will learn to endeavor

Hard work is a part of life,

They fought with all their might for our civil rights

This President tried to take this Country to new heights.

John F. Kennedy (1961-1963)

They are forty something now living their best life

Dealing with the politics in strife

Loving their family instilling education,

vacation, and family relations

Who was the President then

Lyndon B. Johnson (1963-1969)

Late forties and very active in their churches,

they loved to visit each other's church and cause confusion you see

They looked so much alike that you had to look twice
It seemed as if you were seeing doubles.

Who is the President that had more than his share of troubles?
Richard Nixon (1969-1974)

Now time is passing and they are getting old and surrounded by grands
Yet they remain bold, taking a stand to keep us grounded and in God's hand
The world is changing it's the seventies now
we all banded together to make a stand

Who was the President during this era?
Gerald Ford (1974-1977)

The seventies are almost over the twins have survived the
seventies and headed for the eighties.
A peanut farmer is running for President
Could he be heaven sent

They voted for him and he won, that son of a gun.
James (Jimmy) Carter (1977-1981)

These sisters were blessed to see their seventies together.

They worked hard and stayed focused

They didn't believe in that hocus pocus

Now who was the President during this time,
Did he do anything to blow our minds?
Ronald Reagan (1981-1989)

Wow we are in the nineties now, these two sisters are still sharp as ever

Despite a few pitfalls, Theresa still making quilts,

Sisters Sharing Garden secrets.

Talking about old times their sister and brothers,

Joe Willie, Dan they called him Pool, Mattie B., Tonsey, and Elijah

Who was the President then?
George H.W. Bush (1989-1993)

The 90's are coming to an end, 2000's are on the way

Computers and cell phones are the thing of the day

They liked to watch T.V. to pass the time

Who was the President that stayed on their mind?
Bill Clinton (1993-2001)

The world is totally different than when they first started out together

Many years ago, in Yellow Pine Alabama. But they look around and they see

teachers, doctors, nurses, writers, bankers, business owners, soldiers,

salespeople, clerks, truck drivers, bus drivers and many more, they all are family, so they just smiled

Who was the President during this time?
George W, Bush (2001-2009)

Whoa and behold black folks dreams have finally become a reality,

The first Black President of the United States of America

Theresa is now ninety-years-old to witness this miracle

sat before the people. She said to me one day

" I can't believe we finally have a black president, Thank God."

Yes of course she cast her vote for him in. (Both Times)

Need I ask who was the President during this time?
Barack H. Obama (2009-2017)

The Queen is now a centennial part of an elite group. She is now 100 still kicking

and moving about, making quilts and tending her plants,

Loving on any one in need of loving.

She said to me one day " this President is one that needs compassion, to be

President you suppose to love your sisters and brothers"

Who is the President now? Donald Trump (2017-2020) -

By: Wanda S. Lewis

Michael Norris
"MaCocoa, the Poet"

Michael Norris' story began in March of 1971, where he was born in Atlanta Georgia. He was six months old when his family moved to Mobile, Alabama where he ended up growing up. In school he enjoyed writing, though he was slow and his spelling was atrocious, (very grateful for spell check). There was once a writing contest which he was told he would have won if it was not for those two factors. During most of his life, there was little chance to still himself enough to pick up the flow and dance the words. The chance to write did not again appear until about thirty years later.

Life's little rollercoaster of a ride skipped rales for the first of many times. This menagerie of Kismet's side roads had set him in a place and circumstance in which his path would cross with a Magna-Cum Laude of writing from a local school.

This chance meeting resparked the writing candle in him. The moment presented itself at a time he had it in spades. He ended up writing over one hundred poems within a few months; he wished he had the chance to write again, though only in a better climate. A book has been put together, (The Poetry Proxy ISBN: 978-1-4568-1018-4) however putting it into body is a challenge. He has a folder filled with enough poems for a second collection. It is on hold for the time being. To write or not to write is not the question, but whose life does it touch and change.

Psalm 91 - Declaration
By Michael Norris

I who dwells in your secret place, O Most High abides in your shadow dearest Almighty.

I say of you, you are my refuge, you are my fortress, you are my God, and in you I trust.

Surely you deliver me from the snare of the fouler and from the noisome pestilence.

You cover me with your feathers and under your wings is my trust: your Truth is my buckler and shield.

I am not afraid of the terror by night nor the arrows that flieth by day nor the pestilences that walketh in darkness; nor the destruction that waisteth in noonday.

A thousand fall at my side and ten thousand at my right hand; it shall not come near me nor harm me.

Only with my eyes shall I behold and see the reward of the wicked.

For I have made you Lord my refuge; you O Most High my habitation; no evil shall befall me, nor any plague come near me nor my dwelling place.

You have given your angels charge over me to keep me in all your ways.

For you gave your angels charge over me to keep you in all my ways, and they bear me up lest I dash my foot against a stone.

I tread upon lions and adders: the young lion and the dragon I trample under my feet.

For you have set your love upon me, therefore I deliver you: I set you up on high, for you have known my name: You call upon me, and I will answer you: I am with you for I am in you: in time of trouble and in time of peace; I deliver you and honor you.

And because you have set your love upon me; you deliver me and set me up on high because you know my name: I call upon you, and you answer me: you are with me for you are in me; in time of trouble and in time of peace; you deliver me and you honor me.

With long life I make you grateful and show you my salvation.

- **Michael Norris**

DISTRACTIONS
By Michael Norris

Distractions, distractions, distractions, this
world is full of distractions.

Distractions, distractions, distractions, even
the distractions have distractions.

We live to be distracted even from the
distractions themselves.

We die distracted.

Are we running to the distractions or
Are we just running from the other?

When we are running from something,
We always run to something.

We live distracted.

We keep distracted from others.
We keep distracted from ourselves.

Distractions are distractions to the
distractions.

Distractions are a distraction for the

distractions.

We are distracted.

We are the distractions.

- **Michael Norris**

The Word
By Michael Norris

There is a word, a very powerful word.

This word is arguably one of the most influential, and
powerful word ever heard.

Though it is of inconsequential in stature and seemingly less to
empower.

It has been credited to the greatest of towers.

In its solitude it contains as great a possibilities as can be
found.

With others as great, if not greater possibilities abound.

This inconsequential minute little tig can bind with the
greatest of bounds that cannot be broken except by the use of itself.

It poses such liberties that confounds the greatest of
imaginations, in mind or on shelf.

It has the ability to make the impossible, possible.
As well as the ability to sure which is possible not only
impossible as well as improbable.

It has turned heroes into broken-down old wretch.

It has also turned the least, the smallest, most improbable, to more than the greatest of heroes could match.

As it looses, it binds.
As it binds, it looses and unwinds.

This vocabulary crease in any language in itself is a extraterrestrial importance.

This idiom of concept can potentially explode in its own extravagance.

By it, wars are caused.
By it, wars are paused.

By it, fantastic horror and death are made.
By it, awesome wonders and lives are saved.

Now by this time one wonders what word and not phrase could have such impact.

What could cause people, time, and events to embark and react?

IF!!

If I can run, if I can stand.
If I laugh, if I cry.

If I act, if nothing I do.

If I risk nothing, if I risk it all.

If I choose your death over mine.

If I choose your life over mine.

If I gain more, if I lose more.

If I lose a friend, If I gain a brother.

If I add this, if I take from that.

If the sky fall, if I rise…

When all is against me and all seems lost.

When by pulling, pushing, dragging, below the ground so frost.

Where there is no more energy, no more strength, no more

hope, or even life to pay the cost…

What if??

What if?!!

- **Michael Norris**

POP
By Michael Norris

Call him Pop.

Call him Gray or Pop.

Don't call him Horace, call him Pop.

She snapped as her irritation, as usual, flared up.

From that moment to this very one, I still call him Pop.

Always working, always building, never still he be.

From before sun up to past sun set little time to rest we see.

At his work or on the house, struggling, stretching, or on bended

knee.

She kept him busier than his job with moments stolen for

slumbers grace given, a time of indulgence flee.

Those are the moments cherished and kept securely.

Young was I and in need of a father figure to follow.

He, in silence care nudged, kept maturity to grow.

As a tender father in remembrance, not of blood, nor by law, I

always recall him as I know.

Even when a wild streak exploded bound, patience he did show.

Many lessons from him engraved within me to grow.

I learned much from him which in my life impacts me still.

To work steady and to work hard till the day's fill.

To commit to one and to hold still.

The beauty of a simple life without the glimmer and frills

The true meaning, of to love with self sacrifice no matter how bitter the pill.

Tila, he loved very much, more than most to another ever could.
He loved her as she loved him with equal sufferings and
sacrifices more than a couple should.
She could not show him as she should.
He, none the less, showed her the only way he could.
He was there for her when she needed him and tried to be there
for her when allowed him would.
Though not in body but in admiration and feelings' countenance
in one, a path traveled.
Gentile in movement but sure to follow through, his life softly
bellowed.
In this life loves argues path was to us as a fellow who has
been P.O.W.'ed
He in silence, of sorts, pushed through such sufferings for us an
example of life to endured.
His silent courage for our valor to be sured.

In tragedy's wave loves mate's path now was gone
Lost was he without his hold, his direction, his reason
Amis a darkness of a head not clear nor reason, another head led
on.
Tossed and turned, adrift on a path longed for and all but
forgotten upon.
Scares, sores, open wounds are left, lessons for us to learn from
and recollect on.

H. W. Gray, Horace Wilson Gray...Pop

All of the good times, all of the bad times, all of the easy times

and all of the hard times, our memories sadly hop.

In our love for him our memories can be mercifully cropped.

For our love for him we, his time with us, lessons learned, he

himself, our caring cannot and will not stop.

As I choose to remember him, I will address him as I know

him...I call him POP.

- **Michael Norris**

   This is lovingly and respectfully for the remembrance of H. W. Gray

STORIES OF MOMENTS
By Michael Norris

Every story has a moment

Every moment has a story

To each story moments are made

To each moment a story is played

Each story in time is carried

Each story moments are unburied

Stories are moments given way,

To those whom it is fray.

Stories are moments to share and to hide

Stories are moments to care and to guide

Each story is different

As each moment is different

Each moment is different

As we each are different

If we were to mix any of the three

Never the same any would be

We each have time

We each have moments

We each have a story

We all have stories

We together are a volume

Do Tell...

- **Michael Norris**

TIME
By Michael Norris

Moment by moment passes

Moment by moment never stands still

As moments passes, time is measured

As time is measured, so is the movement of

things.

Things are done

Things are undone

Through time matter is seen

Through time more is not seen

By time information is shared

By time information is never lost but always

Glared

From time much needs to be done

From time much more needs to be done

Once time comes it always comes

Once it goes it is forever gone

It is always coming

It always going

Memories are never lost
Memories should always remember the cost

Times made and information share
Times made and memories cared

Memories are to be dearly cherished
Memories as time if not cared always perish
Time is to be precious to the doing without
memories

Memories are to precious to the being without the
sharing

Staying busy in time is fine
Staying busy in time without memories is a
 waste of time

Don't waste memories!

Don't waste time!

-   *Michael Norris*

Nonnie Parker

Nonnie Parker was born in North Mobile County and raised in the town of Mt. Vernon, Alabama to parents of the late Archie & Ophelia Olds. She is the youngest of five siblings and mother of four beautiful children: Vincent, Valencia, Vanity and Vandross. Also, she is the proud grandmother of the most precious granddaughters and charming grandsons. She is currently an instructional paraprofessional for the school system and program assistant for Boys & Girls Clubs of South Alabama.

Nonnie's passion for the Fine Arts begin in her early years, where she spent most of her time reading, writing, acting, reciting poetry, speeches, scripts for school plays and church occasions, as well as, enjoying the outdoors with family and friends. Her biggest motivation for writing is to express personal experiences, the involvement with the youth and community, knowledge of historical and global events. Writing has become her building foundation of encouragement for self and others. Throughout life, Nonnie realized her poems, inspirational quotes and creative writing are a therapeutic talent that is definitely worth sharing with the world in an effort to make a difference.

There's Nothing Sweeter Than A Mother's Love
By Nonnie Parker

There is nothing sweeter than a mother's love
Mother, you planted your seed from Heaven above
You inspired us all to become great men and women
Your daily prayers and strength tripled by seven.

It is because of you, my faith is even stronger
I am going to work even harder and a little bit longer
Mother, what you instill inside of me can't be taken away
Your love, guidance and strength are with me everyday.

My only desire is to become beautiful as my mother
You possess both external and internal beauty
Throughout the years you have touched so many
Your kind, gentle, and sweet spirit was more than plenty.

Mother, you are an inspirational treasure
Your love will never fade; It will last forever
Therefore, it gives me great pleasure to say
Have a Blessed and Happy Mother's Day!

But wait! Please just don't stop right there
Sing praises unto the Lord each and everywhere
Let him know we are thankful for whatever times he gives
It is because of Jesus that our Savior lives.

Happy Mother's Day to All
From the Mt. Calvary Matrons

Written by
©Nonnie Parker 2006

Break Away
By Nonnie Parker

Screaming is anyone listening

I am overworked and underpaid

I do more work than you ever done in a day

Yet, still no pay raise.

Looking down on me because of your degree

You make mistakes and I get blamed

You always looking for an excuse

Ever consider why people really don't want to work with you.

I paid my dues

I did my time

I am removing myself from this do this and do that line

Let see how much you will accomplish before nine.

I wished it could have been resolved

I never intended on leaving this job

Too much of that same dried out tune

So, saying goodbye want be that hard.

©2021einnonrekrap

God Saved Me
By Nonnie Parker

God saved me
From all dangers, toils and snares
God saved me
From all deceitful looks and unpleasant stares.

God saved me
Lord, let your will be done
Give me a new mind, body and soul
Lift my spirit and let my heart be reborn.

God saved me
When others turned away and left
It was you, Lord who held me
In spite of all the misery I felt.

When I felt like doing wrong
It was you who made me do right
God saved me
Making me a better person than I use to be.

God saved me
Once, I opened my heart and accepted you
God saved me
He walks beside me and carries me too.

Seasons and Circumstances may change
Sometimes, family and friends will too
But the love of the Lord will never change
God saved me and he'll do the same for you!

©Einnonrekrap68

Faithfulness in Work
By Nonnie Parker

Faith without work is dead

This is what God said.

Put your faithfulness in your work and see

May the works I've done speak for me.

Faith and work goes hand in hand

Give unselfishly to the sick, the poor, the elderly and the fellow man.

Let not your work be in vain

Let not your faith become tarnish or stain.

Faith is stronger when you put forth the work

In God's Kingdom, you will no longer have to search.

Your work is being recorded and stored too

God knows the value of you work and the amount you do.

©2022einnonrekrap

Hope & Unity
By Nonnie Parker

Hope has kept us united for so many years

Hope has washed away a shipload of tears

We have remained strong in times of uncertainty

We continued to lift our voices because of God's blessings.

We have faced many tribulations and weathered the storms

We survived darkness because God protected us in his arms

Our faith and love for Christ have kept us united

Never in a million years, we will ever deny it.

Hope and Unity goes hand in hand

We pray others will soon begin to understand

We are all on borrowed land and time

We lean and depend on God to keep us in line.

Let us continue to hold on to the promises of God

He has been with us from the very start

God is our source of hope when in despair

God requires his children's united obedience everywhere.

©2021einnonrekrap

Oh, How I Love Thee
By Nonnie Parker

Oh, How Do I Love Thee

Equipped by such flattery

Who truly understands me,

As I elude my misery.

Let me count the ways

Lonely nights and blistering hot days

Am I unworthy of any accolades,

Or fashion fitted for pure outrage.

Oh, How I love thee

Blindsided by the sweet pillow talks

Long drives and breezy beach walks

Hiding like teenagers afraid of getting caught.

Let me count the ways

Curling up to a good book

Sharing the secrets of the greatest cooks

Glancing over for another impromptu look.

Oh, How I love thee

Let me count the ways

Priceless memories of our family

Standing on the promises of better days ahead. - ©2021einnonrekrap

Cynthia R. Poe

Cynthia R. Poe is a longtime member of Spoken Word of Mobile. She is employed as a cashier and she has her own Podcast called "Cynthia's Podcast." Her podcast can be heard on ANCHOR and SPOTIFY.

Cynthia loves being light and meeting people; listening and talking to them, making their day and yes, even learning from them. A lesson my parents taught me; "You are just as good as anybody else!"

Her hobbies are reading, dancing and watching a good lifetime movie to unwind. I really do get high on life. I am from Mobile, Alabama.

Her favorite Bible verse: 23rd Psalm.

When Life Throws You a Curve
By Cynthia R. Poe

When life throws you a curve, catch it. There is going to be obstacles in your way as well as stumbling blocks; you just have to push them out of your way and keep trying. Life is not always going to be straight and narrow. Sometimes it's going to be broad and curvy. Things are not always going to go the way you want them to go. See when life throws you a curve, go around it and shake it off; because it will eventually straighten itself out, not today, not tomorrow but it will gradually work itself out. So remember when life throws you a curve; what are you going to do? Catch it...

"When Life Throws You a Curve."

-   *Cynthia R. Poe*

The History of Highway 45
By Cynthia R. Poe

I remember or should I say I vaguely remember a little about 45. I remember once upon a time the Harlem Duke Social Club was known for its famous down home acts. It housed some of the Blues most prestigious people.

I was a very young girl back then, but I remember the famous sign and passing by the club riding in my parents car. Going there with my sister. I also remember the Carver Theatre. I actually remember going there with her sister to see a movie. I never liked the movies that were shown there.

45 was also known for its famous "overpass" called the "Viaduct." That overpass was so scary going over. It had its share of problems just like some of us; always in need of repair. Those are some of the memories coming from this very young mind of Hwy 45 aka St. Stephens Road in Mobile, Alabama.

Driving in the area now, you would never know that it used to be that way but Time brings about a change in this case. I guess you can say it was for the better or can you? "Go Figure."

- **Cynthia R. Poem Sun. 06/16/16**

The Culinary Brothers
Bro Mitchell & Bro Wallace Poe
By Cynthia R. Poe

My father and his brother, which was Uncle Nick, "let me put it this way;" those men knew their way around the kitchen. They dibber and dab in anything when it comes to food. From peanut brittle to rum balls and not to mention, those homemade hot Texas chili peppers. Back in the day when I was growing up tea cakes were popular with my good ole Dad. Now his stuff, they say, was scrumptious and delicious and his was homemade in a black old fashioned skillet. Alga peanut brittle was to die for. One Christmas my Uncle sent our family a care package made up of rum balls, hot chili peppers and whatever else he threw in that was edible. They were so good plus their game for credit.

I wish they had their own cookbook. Did I mention my dad used to roast the best peanuts that will put the A&M peanut shop to shame?

-   *Cynthia R. Poe*

Things That Go Bump, In The Night
By Cynthia R. Poe

On the night of Hurricane Frederic, my mother and father and I were getting ready to welcome the storm. It was a real bumpy night. Earlier that day, my dad, being the man that he was, made sure we had sheetrock and plywood. My dad was so good about boarding up our picture window with duct tape. Even though there was a storm heading our way, but, I felt safe knowing my dad was around. We never went to a shelter. My brother Ronald did, he got scared and went to the church for shelter. And he ended up back at home because the storm damaged the church. We tried to get him to stay with us, but he wouldn't listen.

Yes our house has been through quite a few hurricanes. My dad always listened to the weather forecast, for as long as we had power. He made sure we had a working flashlight. My mother made sure we kept kerosene oil in the lamps, just in case the lights went out. Me, my mom and dad rode out quite a few storms. My advice to you doing this hurricane season is to be ready......

- *Cynthia R. Poe*

Ghost Street
By Cynthia R. Poe

I was on my way home from work, it was not quite dark yet. The traffic was heavy as usual or for lack of better word congested. I had to stop at Walmart, before I turned into the parking lot. I had a sudden thought or should I say a flashback. I was thinking about all the people including my parents, my brothers who have either drove, walked or at least made this thoroughfare better known as I-65 service road, a familiar hang out spot or perhaps it was someone's way home or just gotta go to Walmart place. The point I am getting at is that a lot of those people are no longer a part of this earthly realm. So, I took that memory a step further, wouldn't it be nice to have had a hidden camera to see all those happy as they looked...then faces. I think that would be awesome, if we could go back in time to capture those images.

Or look through the lens of life moment frozen in time. Memories, reflections of the way it was from the expressions of timeless faces that once crowded the streets, which will only be part of a very special place... will always be with us locked in time, in which I call Ghost Street.

- *Cynthia R. Poe*

Tiffany Pogue

Tiffany Pogue is a photographer, artist, mental health advocate, mentor, and native to Mobile, Alabama. She is an alumni of the University of South Alabama, holding a Bachelor's degree in Psychology with a minor in Sociology. As a half-Filipino descendant of the Clotilda Slave Ship Survivors, she honors the legacy of her ancestors in everything she does.

She has a strong passion for serving her community. She attributes a lot of her influence to the Boys & Girls Clubs of South Alabama - where she has held many different titles over 5 years, including being the Social Media Director at the age of 21. She is the founder and co-creator of the Boys & Girls Clubs of South Alabama's Annual Advocates for Girls Conference - where young girls can learn from women in the community, and the women can learn from these young girls, she serves as an Executive Board Member for Stand Up Mobile - where she advocates for voter education, especially towards young adults.

Her poetry journey began in 2020, while attending her first open mic night in Atlanta, GA, where she boldly decided to read one of her journal entries to the audience, which she later entitled "Listen More." Since then, she fell in love with the art of poetry and began regularly attending spoken word events, like Spoken Word of Mobile.

Listen More
By Tiffany Pogue

I heard a quote that said
"Seek first to understand, then to be understood."
So I decided
to speak less
and listen more.
But simply listening is a hard task
when you have so much to say,
but I'm learning.

Asking more questions,
allowing myself to receive more of the answer.

I can see myself living out everything I wanted to do when I was younger,
but now I know
that's only because
I have a strong support system
and the knowledge that I create my reality.

I'm grateful for the timeline that has unfolded for me.
I don't put very much effort into figuring it all out,
because I know that my only job
is to decide if I'm going to walk through this door of opportunity
or not.

Everyday
I'm faced with yes or no questions that impacts my life forever.
Lately, I've been comparing my life to that of a tree.
Each day, a tree decides which direction it's going to grow in.
The environment might influence it to grow in a certain way,
or prevent it from achieving its full potential.
But at the end of the day, it's choices define how it looks.
The same can be said about our lives. Our choices define our reality.

Since we are limited by the knowledge of our environment, we may never know the
capacity of our true potential.

My greatest fear
is settling for a life that doesn't serve my greater purpose.
I see so many people settling for what they don't want
for the benefit of everyone else.
It makes me sad.

The world would be so much more aligned if we all chose our own growth over the satisfaction of another, or even the satisfaction of our own ego.

I imagine a world where we could meet more people who encourage our personal growth, because they are growing themselves.

But I know that the only way to change the world is to change myself. So I'll just keep listening to what resonates and speaking with intention.

- **Tiffany Pogue**

Lineage
By Tiffany Pogue

Thank your ancestors for persevering so that you may exist.

I come from a black man who transitioned before he could see his youngest turn 2.
I miss the moments we never got to have.
You never got to see my greatest accomplishments
Or feel how beautiful my energy is
Or show me what love truly means to you

All I yearn for is someone to understand me the way I know you would have
But now, instead of watching me grow from your physical form
You view through my mind's eye
I see you sending angels guiding me towards my purpose
I thank you for persevering so that I may exist.

I come from a Filipino woman who was raised on a farm
She didn't have much, and sometimes went to bed hungry
But you always sought better for your life
With little education, money, and trust
You did everything in your power to balance
immigration to America
Four young kids
And the death of your love

So you grew strong
But with all strength comes weakness
You lost the ability to show up emotionally
Because if you did, you'd probably break down and lose it all
I absorbed this
I watched as you carried the world on your shoulders
And I want you to know that you know that you don't have to do that anymore
You've come so far both literally and metaphorically
And I thank you for persevering so that we may exist

I'm not sorry to say this but
None of this shit matters
You know what does matter?
Your reaction to the action you experience
Pay attention to the tension because it's there for a reason
It's here to teach you a lesson about something you may not see
Sometimes we get so caught up in the worries of our thoughts that
We forget we are divinity embodied

Close your eyes with me
I want you to envision the best life you could possibly live
Tell me about it
Now thank yourself for persevering because your future lineage is already grateful
Because it's not about what you think about
It's about what you be about
So think about it

- **Tiffany Pogue**

It Could've Been Me
By Tiffany Pogue

On June 22nd,
I went the memorial service of a boy I barely knew
We interacted a few times at the boys and girls club but I don't think we've ever really
had a conversation
We were completely different but similar in so many ways
They spoke about
How bright he was
How kind he was
How he had so much potential
And all I kept thinking was
That could've been me

Going to a pool party
Just to have fun
Somebody rolls up with a malicious agenda
Now I'm bleeding out
And someone's screaming to call 911
breathe

Man I just can't stop thinking about how
That could've been me
We were alike in so many ways
We both grew up in the BGC
We both got our first job there
We both went on those college trips
And got scolded by our mentors
And had plans to do something better for ourselves and our people
And

I wonder how we got here
Seeing death after death
Seeing potential snatched away by the simple pull of a trigger
And I just can't get over how
that could have been me
Or my brother
Or my cousin
Or my friend
But it wasn't me
It was Isaiah Dickerson
And Anisa Baker
And so so many others
Whose dreams
Emotions

Thoughts
And existence
Were halted by another human being
Who was so insecure with themselves
That they'd rather release their pent up aggression by taking someone else's life than
asking themselves
"What unresolved trauma did they just trigger in me?"
breathe

But maybe my perspective is unfair to these murders
Because who would've taught them how to manage their mental health?
At what point were they going to learn that
We're all just mirrors of each other
And not to take anything personal
Because we're all just doing the best we can based on what we know
Who was going to show them what it truly means to have power?
Not the education system
Not the workforce
And DEFINITELY not their parents
breathe

We're in this karmic cycle of
pain and revenge
And pain
And revenge
And pain
And who's going to break the cycle
breathe

I don't know
I just keep thinking
That could've been me

-   **Tiffany Pogue**

Daron Ray

Daron Ray Sr. is a graduate of John L Leflore class of 83. While attending John L Leflore, he was co-captain his junior year, and captain his senior year. Daron is a veteran of the United States Navy, where he served as a Corpsman in emergency medicine at Charleston Naval Hospital, and Charleston Air Force Base. In 1993 Daron was selected Mr. Bishop State by the student body. In 2014, Daron enrolled at Faulkner State Community College, where he joined Faulkner's State National Honor Society, graduating Summa Cum Laude with an Associate in Arts in 2016. Immediately after Graduation, Daron went on to the University of South Alabama, where he graduated in the top eighty percent of his class in 2019. In 2022 Daron entered the University of South Alabama graduate program where he plans to further learn more about the writing process while earning his Master's in English with a Concentration in Creative Writing. Daron is married and has seven children, who all support him in his writing.

Daron joined Spoken Word of Mobile to be a part of something bigger, and to find his voice on stage. Although Daron is new to Spoken Word, the group welcomed him in as if he had been a part of them throughout the group's twenty-year lifespan. Daron has been writing for over thirty years, writing and releasing the pain that followed him like shadows in the dark. Daron plans to graduate with honors, and if it is the Lord's will, pursue an active life in writing.

Traditions
By Daron Ray

Traditions are now a thing of the past

You can see it in our youth

They are growing up way too fast

It once was a time, it took the entire village

Just to raise one child

Now there are fewer and fewer children

Walking down the graduation aisle

It once was a time

Children were in

Before the streetlights came on

Motherhood has given way

The children are lost and think they are grown

Children are overlooked while doing mischievous deeds

Children raising children unaware of their own needs

It once took a village just to raise one child

Now the village has become laid back

And now has become mild

Our children are acting a little way too grown

Now we villagers are standing idle, watching,

scared to let it be known

In times like these, we need our village

As I look around

The mothers and fathers have made their decisions

And decided to move on

Motherhood has seemed

To have lost its way

And it's our children

Who has that terrible price to pay!

The world needs to turn over

What seems to be a new leaf!

In our village seems we have lost

our one, and only true chief

Spare the rod, spoil the child was

not just a custom, but also a belief

In our homes, we try to be the friend,

there are too many Indians,

in our homes, we are lacking a real Chief

Seems traditions are now a thing of the past

You can see it in our youth

How they are growing up a little way too fast

Lord, we must slow down and stop this selfish greed

Lord, you know our hearts

And you know our needs

Let's sharpen our eyes as if we have a file

let me close by saying,

"We need to understand it takes an entire village

Just to raise one child."

In God We Trust
By Daron Ray

In God, we trust

Your problems.

You don't even have to touch

No more tic, no more tat

No more, you get me, and I get you right back

Because in God, we trust

Your problems,

rest assured you don't even have to touch.

The Search
By Daron Ray

A child is born both here and now,

its nourishment is not milked from a cow

But scripture embedded in its youth

the child grows old and now seeks the truth

Problems arose both dusk and both dark

but let the truth be told as we embark

There are children raising children with

pedophilia's lurking in the mist

Its parents every day who

put our children at that risk

Trying to substitute hardship with relationship, on

each, and every new date

And. it's our children who become victims of

that sad crime we call rape.

Blinded
By Daron Ray

I was going through life

Like bullets out of a gun,

Laughing and loving

having my childhood fun

Not knowing the impact

I had on those who were

all around me

I could not see the forest

I was blinded by the world,

I was blinded by the trees

My life was on overdrive,

I lived like a scavenger

A scavenger on the run,

I was going through life

Like bullets from a gun

My elders all told me

How I needed to settle down

But life was my kingdom

And I enjoyed my crown

I lied, stole, and I also cheated

I cheated just to get to that place

That place we call the top

Stepping on those whom I knew

would help me not!

But God has his way

He knows just how

How to settle you down

Because the same ones

I stepped on going up

I had to beg their forgiveness

As I had to pass them while

I was on my way

down.

Don't Fault Me
By Daron Ray

Don't fault me; it's your choice to be whatever you want to be,

Don't fault me; no one's perfect you see

Don't fault me; I'm not perfect; I made my mistakes

Live your life; follow your dreams, fulfill what is to be your destiny

Don't fault me; I know life is not all about give, and take

Don't fault me; I'm sorry, I know I made my mistakes

Don't fault me; I wish you well.

Don't fault me; I'm sorry I know I put you thru hell

Don't fault me because the apples have soured on your tree,

Don't fault me; God is keeping my every account

And he alone

Will judge me.

Bondage
By Daron Ray

Let's look back on the bondage

How we were brought from Africa as one package

Bought and sold, sold and bought

Some tried to escape soon to be caught

Dragged back by our hands and by our feet

Begging the Lord, Lord, please

Remove me, from this life I'm in

According to them being Black is a sin

I know, that they are deadly wrong

They should have left us where we belong

The knowledge to know that I am somebody too

Be it, Black, white, Japanese, or Jew

If I can find Christ, then so can you.

Preparation
By Daron Ray

Preparation and determination

is the key to one's escalation

It is the motor for even higher acceleration

The actual, the factual not

the dressed-up lies,

or untold truth, hidden and

often well-disguised.

Preparation and determination is the path that

many have chosen but few have completed

The absence of either is

for one's intentions to fall short,

and all his or her dreams,

hopes, and possibilities

to be ransacked and being

cheated!

Cassondra Sims

Cassondra Sims, daughter of Cassandra and Micheal Dumas, is the only sister to the three brothers. She is the mother of four handsome intelligent God-fearing young boys.

She is a Certified Clinical Medical Assistant, and Certified Nursing Assistant, and Licensed Insurance Agent!! She also serves our community as a Licensed Cosmetologist with a minor in Business. Cassondra is very passionate about public speaking, inspiring and uplifting the word of God to the people of God!

Cassondra is a member of the AIM Ministry! And she is very pleased to share some of her personal message, "My purpose is to follow the divine will of God for my life!! I enjoy sharing and listening to poetry in my spare time." She has been excited to share poetry with the rest of the world for some time and very committed to getting the message of the Spoken Word out to as many people that I can reach in my local community. "I am committed and thankful to Spoken Word of Mobile. Thanks to Barefoot Poet, Delores Gibson for the invitation to Spoken Word of Mobile." Cassondra has been a member of Spoken Word of Mobile since at least 2012.

Let Love
By Cassondra Sims

Let the love of GOD surround your soul

with a place that only GOD and heaven holds

Let love and peace capture your life;

to know regardless of the hell on the outside

remember you are the light.

Let the love of joy be a divine guiding light by night,

to know that in the morning everything will be all right.

Let the love of grace and mercy give you life;

to know that with repentance our sins are forgiven; and we have another chance

to make it in the kingdom of GOD with JESUS CHRIST!

-   *Cassondra Sims* **March 14, 2013**

Blindside
By Cassondra Sims

So, what is your blindside you say?
I would say my blindside could be described in so many ways.

Let me start by saying I was born blind as a baby:
Not certain of my life, my future nor my maybes.

As a child I often felt used, sexually abused and out of place.
I was rejected by many from the very beginning.

Now you see me, now you don't
You think you know me, but you really don't.

I never felt I was treated like a little girl;
But I was always called that fast ass lil girl.

Why? Was it because I didn't have ponytails falling down my back;
Or was it because my body was just too stacked?

But that's just me blindsided by what you make of me.
I grew up so fast, I always tried to do good;

But then chose to be bad.
That was expected of me;

That's just that look I had
.
I always wanted to fit in but I simply stood out.

I was considered a loudmouth with a bold personality so it was always my fault.

But again It's just me; blindsided by what you say about me.

I was just a flirt but called a freak. I could never get freaky because of some of the
things that had happened to me.

I was called a whore, but I never really even like to cheat. I just thought love looked
better on me.

I was always broken hearted and wanting love to stay; but love wasn't real,

So that's just the price I had to pay

I'm always giving, and people always just take.
Take my love for granted.

But that's just me blindsided by my mistakes.

So, you ask what I am leading to or what am I trying to say.

I am saying I thank God for my blindside;

Because it has molded and prepared me into the woman I am today.

My life hasn't been so bad and I'm having some great times along my way.

I'll just say my life is a mirror you might see broken but I see it much clearer.

See I am no longer that desperate little girl. Nor that shallow young lady who needs to
be loved

And accepted by the world; to only be misplaced and mistaken.

I show myself to be friendly and then to not have a friend.

I show myself a lover and then turn around and not have a man.

I show myself standing tall and then only feel so very small.
I show myself to be a warrior and a survivor then I turn around and not fight at all.

I show myself standing still and then all of a sudden take a fall.
But My GOD is and was there through it All.

To show me a real and true friend.
To show me an honest and God-fearing man.

To show me how to be bold and fearless at all times.
To show me how to always stand tall and to never feel small and how to fight fight fight
through it All.

So, it was ok to be blindsided by what I thought I saw, just to know that the Good
LORD's love and mercy is always leading and following me

- **Cassondra Sims, August 2013**

Mama's Big Shoes
By Cassondra Sims

As a little girl I loved putting on my mama high heel shoes and,

My brother would always say: "Girl, you can't wear mama shoes."

But me: "Boy, shut up! Uh, I'm not gonna just wear mama high heels shoes but, I'm

gonna rock mama outfit too..."

My brother: "Girl, you are not grown."

Me: "Boy, I'm growner than you!"

Mama: "I tell you what then! How about you go to work, and pay all these bills too, wash

the clothes, and the dishes then cook the food too, clean the bathrooms and then help

your brother with his homework too. "

Me: "Hold up Mama, I can't wear your shoes."

My brother: "Girl, I told you, you are not grown and them shoes are too big for you."

- **Cassondra Sims, September 2014**

You Don't Know Me
By Cassondra Sims

Who is it that you think you knew that little sassy girl name with an attitude;

Or that skinny bald head girl with that Jheri curl?

Big booty, hips and thighs all that at the age of 5;

With baggy eyes and big horse teeth

Oh yeah, those were some of the names y'all called Me.

I was molested at the age of 6; talked down on and sometimes mistreated too.

So, who is it that you think you knew?

They would say; "she's so damn grown, her little fast ass; you know that little bitch

makes me sick; I bet when she grows up, she ain't gonna be shit."

So who is it that you think you knew?

I started smoking weed and drinking when I was 11.

Then, Lord touched me at the age of 12; and that was my escape from hell.

That touch was the best feeling I have ever felt and has forever changed my life;

Then I began witnessing and telling everybody about the love of Jesus Christ.

Some listened, some were saved too, some cast me down and said "you hypocrite you."

So, who is it that you think you knew?

Yes, I have sin, and I still fall short of GOD'S glory too.

And I used to sell weed at the age of 15 and I tried selling crack too.

I dropped out of school when I was in the 11th and it was not because I had a

miscarriage.

So, who is it you think you know?

Now y'all smile in my face and say, "I'm so proud of you."

Why? Is it because y'all prejudged me?

Well guess what, I am so proud of y'all too.

Because y'all are the people who grew to know the little girl,

The young lady, the woman I always knew!

But y'all still persecute and reject me

And don't want to face the truth.

And yes, I love and forgive you all. See I was chosen for this very cause.

Now I can see why y'all are so proud of me,

It's because I overcame all the names, all the false blames,

The misuse and the sexual abuse. I'm no longer ashamed of all those things.

Now I embrace my past. No Pain, No Gain.

I thank GOD for my past because my past made my future so bright;

My future was guarded by GOD'S guiding light.

See, when GOD touched me, HE brought me back into remembrance when HE died

then rose in 3 days with all power in HIS hands. See what y'all didn't know I WAS

BORN TO WIN!!

Because My Father is the Alpha and Omega. HE Is the Beginning and the End.

The almighty King, I know it seems impossible Me Fatso, Cassondra a Queen, a wife, a

mother, a server, a chief, a counselor, a nurse, a teacher, a stylist, a designer, a writer,

a poetess, a witness, and a speaker. Oh yes, I Am a true believer! Really, Me,

Cassondra Fatso up surged you all see; but I told y'all

Y'ALL DON'T KNOW ME!!!

-   **Cassondra Sims, December 1, 2012**

I'm Mad at My Mama
By Cassondra Sims

I'm mad at my mama, that's why I got an attitude;

I'm mad at my mama, but I'm not gonna let it give me the blues.

I'm mad at my mama, because of the things she do;

I'm mad at my mama, but I know she's human too,

I'm mad at my mama, because she never make time for me;

I'm mad at my mama, because she chooses the casino over me

I'm mad at my mama, because she doesn't seem to care how I feel;

I'm mad at my mama, because she's gonna come around me

when I make those mills$$.

I'm mad at my mama, even though sometimes we are really close;

I'm mad at my mama, and I can't wait until we both receive the gift of the Holy Ghost.

I'm mad at my mama. because I don't want her to let our bond go;

I'm mad at my mama, even though she always tells me she loves me so.

I'm mad at my mama. because I want her to be my best friend in so many ways;

I'm mad at my mama, but in my heart is where she will always stay.

I'm mad at my mama, but not for real

I love my mama!

- **Cassondra Sims, December 2011**

Sarah "BOAZ" Szejniuk

On the day of August 3, 1971 in Montgomery, AL at St. Margaret's Hospital a healthy bouncing baby girl named Sarah Leah Szejniuk was born. I was born to the parents of Noach Motel Szejniuk and Doris Jean (Messenger) Szejniuk (both are now deceased). I'm the youngest of 3 siblings. I have a brother and sister, nieces, nephews, and other extended family. I have worked at being a caretaker and I'm always helping others (if and when I can), I also sold Avon for awhile until I had to quit due to unforeseen circumstances took place in my life. I have lived in various places all my life. Some places have been fun and interesting and well, some places have been a real challenge (for those of you who know what I mean). Although, my life has had it's fair share of ups and downs. I can honestly say that my faith in God has brought me through alot.

Growing up I was always creative with everything that I would have.I would go to the library and read all kinds of poetry books. There were times that you would have to pry me out of the library, simply because I didn't want to leave. Sometimes, I would check out so many poetry books that I would need a basket, a cart or something to carry them in. There are always people, places, situations, and things that are inspiring to me. I just have to write it down and put it all together and maybe one day I could have a book or a series of books to publish and share with everyone. Also, I have a brother who is a poet and short story writer and co-authored a poetry book called "Freedom Through Poetry."

Have You Thought about ME?
By Sarah "BOAZ" Szejniuk

Have you thought about me?

Have you thought about how I'm doing?

Am I sick or am I well? Have I died or am I alive?

Have you thought about me?

Have you thought about where I am?

Am I safe and protected or am I in danger;

and frightened.

Have you thought about me?

Have you thought about what I desire, want or need?

Have you thought about me?

Have you thought about my feelings, hopes and dreams?

Have you thought about me?

© *Sarah Szejniuk 7/3/19*

After having a conversation with my brother.

Patches
By Sarah Szejniuk

Patches of Red, Green and Blue,
Patches, my friend where are you?
When you died and went away,
I started to leave but decided to stay.

Patches, I can't believe you are gone;
For the days are short and the nights are long.
Rest in Peace, my dear friend.
Patches, I'll love you always!

Originally written by my mother, to her very close friend who passed away.

Take Time
By Sarah Szejniuk

Take time my friend to talk to God;

He hears our every word.

He seeks and speaks to us in ways that can't be heard.

He walks and talks with us each day

And is never very far away

This was originally written by my mother a long time ago.

PASSING THROUGH
By Sarah Szejniuk

I expect to pass through this world but once.
Any good thing, therefore, that I can do or any kindness
That I can show to any fellow creature, let me do it now;
Let me not defer or neglect it, for I shall not pass this way again.

I have adapted this poem by my family friend, Mollie Stewart, who passed away just before her 103rd birthday.

Geneo Williams

From the fertile soil of the Campground, thru many welcoming doors of the Mobile County Public School System, He come. He began creating poems in the early 70s. The poems that were created appeared in local newspapers and magazines. Ace Newspaper, Inner City News, Mobile Beacon, The New Times. In collaboration with local artists, an assortment of poetry cards were distributed and sold during the early 70s and 80s. After the departure of Spoken Word of Mobiles' founder Cheryl "CJ" Jones, Geneo began hosting Spoken Word monthly gatherings at the Virginia Dillard Smith/Toulminville Branch Library. During this time, numerous expressive faces graced the room resulting in dramatic, fulfilling, exciting presentations; leaving an indelible mark upon the lovers of poetry within the Mobile community. Kudos to the members of Spoken Word of Mobile for a job well done.

From the rough, tough, unforgettable treacherous streets I come; thru bleak sometimes neat Campground Community of Mobile Alabama. Amongst dedicated school servants who refused to let us fail.

Writing to verbalize, to internalize, to express, to remember, to forgive, to forget, to acknowledge, to digest. Words.

Parting Ways
By Geneo Williams

The Jazz Lady,
Left me the other day.

She said,
"I didn't know how to thump anymore"

She said,
"I didn't know how to blow her horn."

She said,
"I didn't know how to tickle her keys."

She said,
"The rhythms is all on me."

She said,
"I sometimes forget to pause."

She said,
"I sometimes forget to bow."

The Jazz Lady,
Left me in the cold.

She said,
"She didn't love me anymore."

The Jazz Lady.
Stood and stepped away.

Letting me,
See her strut her stuff.

She gave,
Me such a marvelous view.

Hey Jazz Lady!
I'm not mad at you

GENEO

Jazzing Out
By Geneo Williams

Lay me down in a big wide coffin
Place a trumpet by my side
Take me onward home to glory
Take me out In Jazzing Style

Let the Saxman take a bow
As he serenades to me
Let the Drumlady beat her pace
As she thump forever free

Let the Pianoman tune his keys
Let the Songstress blare carefree
For the order of the day
Is to do this thing for me

Let them step and strut and profile
Let them style and sway with glee
For the order of the day
Is to do this thing for me

That you do this thing for me
That you do this thing for me
For the order of the day
Is to do this thing for me

When they see the band approaching
When they hear the blaring sound
They will all come a' running
To see what it's all about

As they stop and turn in sequence
To the rhythm of the beat
And smile and wave both hands
With the stomping of the feet

That you do this thing for me
That you do this thing for me
For the order of the day
Is to do this thing for me

GENEO

Offensive Stride
By Geneo Williams

When you have the resources
And the control___you can pull up
stakes and relocate a medical
facility wherever you please.

When you have the resources
and the control___you can place
a shopping center in the middle of
nowhere and build up the surrounding area.

When you have the resources
and the control___you can designate
appointments, ethical or otherwise
not caring about critical reaction.

When you have the resources
and the control___you can make
unwarranted statements, unjust
accusations for reactionary purposes.

When you have the resources
and the control___you can have good
men bowing, nice ladies clawing
for rough face.

When you have the resources
and the control___you can take
flight, even in broad daylight,
when a situation becomes
too hot and heavy.

When you have the resources
and the control___people, values
and ideas are of secondary concern;
since the central attraction is
always you.

GENEO

James Williams, Jr.

James Williams, Jr. is a Mobile, Alabama native. He is a long serving member of his community, as a very active member of his church and as a former law enforcement officer.

James has been writing poetry since early in his childhood. He has been a long-time member of Spoken Word of Mobile. In 2017, he began to compile his writings from journals and personal notes. In 2019 he published his first poetry collection, <u>The Book of James</u>.

He is very excited to be a part of this anthology, along with his friends and follow poets from Spoken Word of Mobile.

Care
By James Williams

I see in your eyes a pain that's deep..

For so long it's relief to seek

As many are healed others find they are left

To suffer in silence or moan at best...

Its in the dead of night...

Horrors and fears

(Won't behave themselves)

(weakens one's will)

For so long some have worn the pain

Others hid the hurt as I came...

Call out his name..

Ask for mercy and comfort too

Think back on your life and future plans...

It's in his will it's nothing you did...

This path was put your way...

Have faith and pray

What can one say or do to loosen the grip placed on you

Physically mentally and spiritually...

Pain is pain...

Testify when it happens to you...

There within strength and weakness resides

What causes us to pick one

And lay the other aside

It's in your hearth....

In your soul what you feel is a goal....

Heaven knows....

If you choose to be weak or

To be strong...

Life's lessons come to us in

Calmness and storms

When it's pain or relief...

We see...

Ourselves or others going through....

It's a blessing in itself...

When others care.

- *James Williams*

There is a Day
By James Williams

There is a day that's set aside

To honor those with endless strives

There are those who give their best

And in return they are blessed

There will be a time of pain

But mother will say

Sunshine comes after the rain

There may be one you sacrifice for

Exposing your heart to the core

There's a friend who never sleeps

He checks mother's every heart beat

There's a way that he can tell

So a mother's love will never fail

There's a world unsodden as can be

And there are mother's in the image of thee.

- *James Williams*

Last and Last
By James Williams

Traveling on a journey that never started

Never ends…perpetual motion destination unknown

A continuous ride held in place by unseen connections

programmed each day

Dark to light you day begins…question why you get up

In a thousand years maybe come back…

Fix wrongs…make that your task

Bound by body …hold dear your soul…we leave here

Each second…in heaven to be or eternally roam

Back and forth we move…anxious we are are…what for?

In a flash it seems things change right before your eyes…

Can't hide

Late at night or just before dawn…

Visiting a place far from the sun

Colorful images hard to describe make their way

Infusing my mind

Sweet is the journey explore your inner world…

Find secrets…mysteries are revealed

Sad sometimes the end most know…faith in a world…

Belief opens that door.

Your experience is just a chemical moment….

Not even a flash yet we do and say.

Last and last.

- *James Williams*

Sponsorships

Spoken Word of Mobile would like to thank our sponsors for bringing about the fulfillment of this project, a long aspired goal of our members. We are very grateful to our sponsors! Thank you very much!

Betty Marks

"Congratulations Spoken Word of Mobile!"

Kibberal Eaton

"Dedicated to Glenda Barney, You are not here with us physically but you are always in our heart and thoughts. Love You Always, Kibberal Eaton and Family."

Cristal Locke

"Congratulations Spoken Word of Mobile!"

Virginia Walker

"In memory of Ray Charles Walker. With love from Virginia, Raydrick, Cali Rose and Kayden Walker"

Fred & Theresa Sullivan

"Congratulations Spoken Word of Mobile and to my sister, Delores Gibson - The Barefooted Poet"

Tammy & Ben Thomas

"Congratulations Spoken Word of Mobile! And to my sister, our aunt, Delores Gibson - The Barefooted Poet. With Love from Tammy, Ben, Tiara, Ty, & Jasmine Thomas"

Larry & Deborah Johnson

"Congratulations Spoken Word of Mobile and to my sister, Delores Gibson - The Barefooted Poet. With Love from Larry, Deborah, Tammy & Kimberly Johnson."

Sponsorships

Spoken Word of Mobile would like to thank our sponsors for bringing about the fulfillment of this project, a long aspired goal of our members. We are very grateful to our sponsors! Thank you very much!

Tyquisha Gibson

Gibson Tax Service: 251-367-6365

"Congratulations, Spoken Word of Mobile & Delores Gibson - The Barefooted Poet from Tyquisha, Troy, Jordan, and Tavares."

Adrienne Gibson

Coko Lush Collection: 251-387-6090

CoKo Lush Collection

"Congratulations Spoken Word of Mobile! And to my Mom/Granny, Delores Gibson - The Barefooted Poet. From Jevon, Adriana, Auriah and Adrienne Gibson."

Painting Healthy Habits

Deidra Craig: 251-391-1843

Bosley Entertainment

Bosley Party Rentals: 251-287-6584

Maki S Gibson

"Congratulations to my mother, Delores Gibson, The Barefoot Poet and Spoken Word of Mobile. And Congratulations Grandmother from Maki, Jeremiah, Zachius, Noah, and Micah Gibson"

Keisha Johnson Pettway

"Congratulations Spoken Word of Mobile! And Congratulations to my Nanny - Delores Gibson, The Barefoot Poet from Keisha Pettway and Mariah Sylvester"

Sponsorships

Spoken Word of Mobile would like to thank our sponsors for bringing about the fulfillment of this project, a long aspired goal of our members. We are very grateful to our sponsors! Thank you very much!

Gertrude Laffiette

"Congratulations Mom, "Peace Maker" & Spoken Word of Mobile on your 20th Year Anthology! Keep on speaking those beautiful words! Love, Alecia Laffiette Johnson"

In memory of Annitta Martin Laffiette

"Congratulations, Gert Laffiette (Peacemaker & Spoken Word of Mobile on your 20th Anniversary Anthology from Pastor J.P. Laffiette Sr. & Pastor Joseph (Tressler) Laffiette II"

Evelyn Gaines & Daron Ray, Jr.

"A kind donation to Spoken Word of Mobile. Congratulations from Daron Ray, Jr. and Evelyn Gaines."

Daniel Cook

BBB Bail Bonds, LLC: 251-405-5577

"Congratulations Spoken Word of Mobile & Aunt Delores Gibson! From Daniel and Tasha Cook and Family."

The Family of Sarah Fields

"A kind donation to Spoken Word of Mobile in memory of Sarah Hester Crawley Fields, from her family."